Blue

Sue Mayfield

Hodder
Children's
Books

a division of Hodder Headline Limited

*To Jo, Nikola, Annwen, Sarah, Jenny, Helen
and Anna, with best wishes and thanks.*

A Catalogue record for this book is available from
the British Library

ISBN 0 340 80519 6

Typeset by Avon Dataset Ltd, Bidford-on-Avon, Warks

Printed and bound in Great Britain by
The Guernsey Press Co. Ltd, Channel Isles

Hodder Children's Books
a division of Hodder Headline Limited
338 Euston Road
London NW1 3BH

1

Anna Goldsmith opens the front door. There is no one home. The morning post is still on the mat. Anna picks it up and puts it by the telephone without looking at it. She dumps her school bag in the hall and hangs up her coat. Sunlight is coming through the front door, casting fingers of light across the floor.

The cat pads towards her, stepping through the pools of light. It rubs itself against her legs. Anna looks in the mirror. Her nose is big, her eyebrows are too bushy. Down her cheeks her eye make-up has run in two dark tracks.

She goes into the kitchen and turns off the dishwasher. Taking a tin of cat food from the cupboard under the sink, she opens it and spoons it into a bowl. The cat purrs and rubs its chin against her arm as she bends down.

Anna switches on the radio. She turns it up so loud that it distorts. Standing on a chair, she reaches up to the shelf and takes down a bottle. She unscrews the lid. On the tablecloth there are toast crumbs and grains of sugar. Anna brushes them away with her hand. Her hand is shaking. She tips the bottle on to the tablecloth and counts the smooth tablets. There are eleven. Carefully, she puts them back into the bottle and puts the bottle in the pocket of her skirt. Her pocket is full of damp tissues. She takes them out and stuffs them into the kitchen bin. She switches off the radio.

The phone rings and Anna jumps. She does not answer it. It rings five times and then the answering machine clicks on. She hears her mother's voice, cheery and crisp: please leave your message after the tone. Then a beep.

Anna goes to the dining-room and opens the cupboard in the dresser. She stares blankly in, fingering the cold bottles. Two bottles of sherry – one sweet, one dry; three bottles of whisky, and an unopened bottle of brandy that they bought on the ferry, duty-free. She reaches to the back and lifts out a bottle of vodka. It is three-quarters full. Anna closes the cupboard. She walks towards the stairs. The cat is stretched out on the mat in the hall, washing its paws. Anna steps past it.

She goes upstairs and into her bedroom and closes the door. She puts the vodka and the bottle of pills on her bed and takes a blue notebook from under her pillow. She takes a pencil from her pencil pot and sharpens it into the bin. The shavings fall in a soft spiral. Anna presses the pencil point into the ball of her finger. It is sharp as a pin. She presses harder until her fingertip turns white. When she takes the pencil away, there is a tiny crater. Anna watches as it disappears.

Then she takes off her school uniform and folds it on her chair. There is a full-length mirror on the wall behind the door. Anna looks at herself in her underwear. She turns sideways. Her bottom is huge. It makes her look like a pear. She turns frontways. There is a mole, the size of a raisin, just above the line of her knickers. Anna puts her finger over it. She pulls a T-shirt from the drawer and puts it on. It is white and extra-large. It comes almost to her knees, like a hospital gown. Anna has a bruise on her left ankle, yellow and black like an overripe banana. She puts on a pair of socks to cover it. She looks at her arms and traces a thin red line with her fingernail. The cat is at the door, mewing softly.

Anna sits on the bed and brushes her hair. When she tips her head forward it tumbles in thick waves, covering her face like a heavy black curtain. Anna takes a cushion from the floor and holds it tightly to her chest. Then she stuffs the corner of it in her mouth and bites hard. She bites until her jaws ache and her cheeks are soaked with tears. Then she takes her sharpened pencil and begins to write.

2

Anna didn't come to orchestra. Mr Brigg looked at the empty chair at the front of the first violins and said, "Where's Anna?"

No one answered.

"She was in school today, wasn't she?" he said.

"She was here in English," said a boy in the cellos.

I sat very still and stared at my music. Then I heard my name.

"Melanie?" Mr Brigg was looking at me hopefully. My stomach began to churn.

"Sir?" I said.

"Anna Goldsmith," he said. "Any idea where she is?"

My palms were suddenly clammy. I laid my clarinet across my knees.

"She went home, sir," I said, "at afternoon break. She wasn't feeling very well . . ."

It wasn't a complete lie. She *had* gone home. I think.

When I got home I phoned her. I got the answering machine. Five minutes later Hayley Parkin phoned me.

"You went a bit over the top, didn't you Melanie?" she said. "Poor Anna!"

I called her a cow and hung up.

Perhaps I should explain. It all goes back a bit, you see. Anna Goldsmith came to our school in Year Nine, that's two and a half years ago. She came just before Christmas. I remember the first time I saw her. It was snowing. The classroom floor was all mucky and wet from snow melting off people's shoes. Anna was sitting in the form room beside the radiator. She had a school blazer on and it looked all stiff and new. None of the girls wear blazers. We just wear black jumpers. I thought she was really beautiful. She's got amazing skin and this wonderful wild hair.

Hayley Parkin swooped in quick and volunteered to look after Anna. She was all over her. Anna this and Anna that.

"This is where we put our bags, Anna. You can use my locker, if you like, until you get a key." . . . "I'll show you the cafeteria, Anna. Oh no, I don't like chips much either, Anna." . . . "So your dad's a doctor, is he Anna? A consultant? Wow!" . . . "Where do you live Anna? Near the park? Oh it's nice there, Anna, isn't it? Are you settling in OK?"

By the end of the week they were inseparable. They sat together in the form room. They got changed next to each other in PE. They whispered together in the cloakroom and linked arms in the corridors. No one else got a look in.

Anna was clever. The teachers liked her. She was good at hockey and walked straight into the team. The coach put her at Centre Forward because she was fast. She moved Hayley to Centre Half. Hayley didn't seem to mind.

Anna was brilliant on the violin and Mr Brigg made her leader of the school orchestra by the end of the Christmas term. She even played a solo in the Christmas concert.

Hayley told everyone how proud she was of Anna: Wasn't Anna talented? Didn't she have fantastic hair? Didn't she speak beautifully?

Anna came from Down South. She said *baaath* and *graaass*. Some of the boys teased her for sounding like the Queen.

"I think Anna sounds lovely," Hayley said. Gradually, Hayley stopped talking with a Yorkshire accent and started to talk like Anna. No one seemed to notice. No one said anything.

Hayley likes to overwhelm people. She likes to buy them things. My mum says her family have more money than sense. Her dad drives a Jag.

Hayley did that with Anna. At the beginning.

She'd buy her sweets at lunchtime and Diet Coke from the machine in the cafeteria. Then it was CDs and bits of jewellery. Then perfume – expensive stuff: Ralph Lauren. The same as Hayley wears. When

Hayley got a new Calvin Klein bag for school she gave Anna her old one. At Christmas she bought her a watch – a really smart one with a metal strap.

Hayley's mum runs a sunbed rental business. She has an all-year-round tan. So has Hayley and so has Hayley's dad. My mum says they'll all end up with skin cancer.

I noticed that Anna started looking tanned too. She went a lovely honey colour. Her skin seemed to glow.

Anna looked happy then. She had sparkly eyes. It seems hard to imagine now . . .

3

Mrs Goldsmith opens the front door. She drops her briefcase on the floor and places a stack of exercise books on the telephone table. Then flopping down into a chair, she prises off her too-tight shoes and rubs her feet.

The telephone rings. She answers it.

"Frances?" a voice says. "I didn't expect to get you. I was all prepared for the robot!"

"Hi Sally!" she says.

"How come you're home already?"

"New shoes!" Frances Goldsmith wriggles her toes as she speaks. "They've been crippling me all day and I couldn't face going round Sainsbury's in them! I've only popped back to change them. It's lucky you caught me. Are we still on for tonight?"

She hooks the phone under her chin and unbuttons her raincoat.

"Eight o'clock OK?" asks Sally.

"Eight sounds fine," she says, tossing the coat on to the chair. "I'll check with Anna when she gets in from orchestra and if there's a change of plan I'll ring you back."

She puts down the phone and glances at the post. Then she listens to the answering machine. There are two messages. The first is David's secretary at the hospital saying sorry, but he'll be late home. The second is Melanie Blackwood saying sorry about this afternoon and will Anna ring her back.

Frances Goldsmith goes into the kitchen. She notices that the cat has been fed and the dishwasher turned off. She goes along the hall and sees that Anna's bag and coat are already there. The house is silent. Going to the foot of the stairs she calls out, "Anna!"

No one answers.

She scribbles a note on the kitchen table:

Dear Anna,
Gone to Sainsbury's, back 6-ish. Get yourself something to eat, if you're starving. Are you in tonight? Daddy and I are due Sally and Mike's 8 pm.
Love you, Mum x

Then she goes to the downstairs loo. The toilet roll is all used up. "Damn!" she says under her breath. "Why does no one else ever think to replace it?"

Frances Goldsmith runs upstairs with her blouse half-tucked in. The loo rolls are in the airing cupboard. The airing cupboard is on the landing, next to the bathroom door. The bathroom door is usually open. She notices that it is closed.

"Anna?" she says again. She knocks on the bathroom door.

She knocks again, louder. There is silence.

She tries the door. It is locked.

"Anna!" she shouts. She hammers on the door with her fist. "Anna, open the door! Anna! Are you in there?"

Suddenly Frances Goldsmith has a hollow feeling in her stomach. She runs downstairs and rummages for the garage key. She unlocks the garage and opens the tool box. Her hands are shaking. She gets a screwdriver. She runs back upstairs.

"Anna!" she shouts. Her voice is charged with panic.

She fumbles with the screwdriver in the bathroom lock. The lock springs free. She puts her weight on the handle and opens the bathroom door . . .

4

Hayley Parkin goes off people. I don't know why. Perhaps she gets bored with them. Perhaps she runs out of things to buy them. Perhaps she can't stand competition. She doesn't seem to need a reason. She just drops people.

She dropped Anna Goldsmith. No one really knew why. Maybe it was the rivalry in hockey. Maybe it was that Anna was cleverer than she was, and worked harder too. Maybe Anna wasn't impressed enough with Hayley's money and her designer gear. Or maybe it was just bad chemistry – one of those things, a personality clash.

Whatever it was, it was bad. I've seen Hayley Parkin turn against people before. People – kids in our year group – try to keep "in" with her. It's been like that since primary school. It's better to be in her gang than out of it. Even some of the boys go along with what she says. She has this knack of making people feel special so that they get a warm glow when they do things that please her. Girls try to dress like her – the Kickers shoes, the Umbro sports gear . . . even the long blonde Hayley Parkin hair. People make a point of liking the same stuff she likes. I've done it too.

Like I say, I've seen her go off people before. But never the way she went off Anna Goldsmith.

At first Hayley just ignored Anna. That was just before the Easter holidays. Hayley changed lockers so that hers was as far away from Anna's as possible. Hayley moved seats in Maths saying that she wanted to be able to see the board better. If Anna was talking, Hayley deliberately turned away and pretended not to hear.

Anna was slow to cotton on. She kept behaving as though they were still friends, standing beside Hayley in the dinner queue and smiling at her and telling her things. On the last day of term Anna asked Hayley if she wanted to go clothes shopping in Leeds in the holidays. We were in the form room. There were loads of people listening. Hayley looked straight at her and said, really loud, "I don't think so, Anna." Then she turned away and smirked.

Anna went to France in the Easter holidays. On the first day back she was telling the French teacher about it. Anna's good at French. Her mum is Head of Modern Languages at a school across town. They go to France most holidays.

Hayley came in and made a point of sitting on the other side of the room from Anna. We could hear what Anna was saying. The teacher was smiling and sucking up to her. The teachers like Anna a lot, especially the men. She has this way of putting her head on one side and flicking her hair back when she's talking to them.

Hayley did a huge yawn and said, "Oh, not France again, Anna!" She said it under her breath, but loud enough for people around her to hear. People smiled.

The lesson started. We opened our text books. It was a passage about making brandy in France. There were pictures of distilleries and enormous wooden barrels.

Anna was at the front of the class. Mr Atkinson asked Anna to read. She read it really well with a proper French accent.

Hayley was at the back. She started taking the mickey out of Anna's pronunciation. She did it discreetly enough for Mr Atkinson not to notice, wiggling her head about and saying in a silly voice, "Ah, oui! Bonjour! Cognac! Ah-ho he-ho!"

People laughed. I laughed too. Hayley looked pleased with herself. People were watching her, waiting for more entertainment.

Then a boy called Joshua joined in. "Merci, Anna!" he said, impersonating Mr Atkinson. "Can I rub-a your teets, Anna?" He said it too loud.

"What's the joke, Joshua?" said Mr Atkinson, looking up.

I caught Hayley's eye and she stared me out.

"That's rather rude, talking and laughing when Anna is reading so beautifully, isn't it Joshua?" Mr Atkinson frowned.

Joshua was moved to a seat nearer the front. Hayley Parkin does that. She starts things and then other people get the blame.

Hayley started picking on Anna a lot that term. But it was subtle, low-key. Some of the things Hayley did and said were so trivial that I can't even remember them. It was something and nothing. But a few things stick out. Hayley would stop talking when Anna came into a room, for example. Or she'd exchange looks with people and smirk and grin just to make Anna feel uncomfortable. Sometimes if Anna tried to join in with conversations she'd say things like, "Sorry, Anna, this is private." Or if Anna was in a group, Hayley might come and take one or two of the group off and say something secretive like, "Excuse me Anna but can I just have a word with Siobhan?" Siobhan or Ruth or Melanie.

Then Hayley started to imitate the way Anna spoke. She'd be standing in the cloakroom and she'd suddenly say, "When I get home I must have a *baaath*!" If Anna looked up she'd say, "Sorry Anna, I was only joking. You know I think your voice is lovely." Then she'd turn away and smile.

In PE she'd make remarks about hairy legs. Anna's

got really dark hair so if she doesn't shave her legs it shows. Hayley would sit near her and say things like, "I must shave my legs tonight. I don't want to look like a gorilla!" Then she'd smirk.

Anna's not fat. She's got a great figure. But she's got quite big hips. One day we were in the form room and Hayley had a fashion magazine. She sat next to Anna to show her some photos. Anna looked surprised that Hayley was talking to her.

"These are nice trousers, aren't they, Anna?" Hayley said. They were wide-legged floaty things. The sort of trousers Hayley would never wear.

"Yeah, they're OK," said Anna.

"They'd suit you, Anna," said Hayley. Anna smiled. Then Hayley said, "They're a good cut for people with big bottoms."

I could see Anna was offended, but she tried to laugh, tried to make it look as though she shared the joke.

After Hayley and Anna fell out, Anna started spending more time with me. I was glad. I liked her. We seemed to be in the same place a lot – in the same sets for all our lessons, both in the hockey team, both in the orchestra. Anna lives quite near me too so we started catching the bus home together. We started to play tennis after school on the courts in the park near where we live. Anna's good at tennis – she had coaching before she moved here. She gave me lots of tips, helped me with my strokes. She made me work on my backhand.

Anna invited me round to her house a lot too. She's got a great bedroom, up in the attic with sloping roofs, and bright blue walls and loads of dangly mobiles. Ikea furniture and orange cushions and a cool CD player.

I like her mum and dad. I like her brother Tom as well. He was in the Lower Sixth then. He's seriously hunky. He'd be in the kitchen with his friends making toast and pop tarts. I could tell some of his friends fancied Anna.

I used to hang around with Helen Burrows, before Anna Goldsmith came. Her mum is friends with my mum. Helen goes to Guides with me and we used to go horse riding on Sunday mornings. Helen's sensible and quiet. She's nice enough, but alongside Anna she seemed so dull and ordinary. And immature too.

I suppose by the end of the summer term Anna Goldsmith was my best friend. Hayley Parkin didn't like that.

5

They reshuffle the forms in our school at the end of Year Nine. It's supposed to mix up groups of friends, freshen the dynamic a bit. It also gives the teachers a chance to split up trouble-makers and isolate people who are dossing too much. Our school is doing well in the league tables. They like us to work hard.

So that people don't end up in a form with no one they know, we have to nominate our two best friends and they try to take that into account when they do the reshuffle. It's supposed to be confidential – like a secret ballot. They give us a piece of paper and no one except the teacher is meant to see what we've written. But it doesn't work like that. Everyone looks over everyone else's shoulder and discusses whose names they're writing down.

Hayley Parkin had a field day. She had decided she didn't want Anna Goldsmith in our form and she set about making sure no one nominated Anna. With most of the class that wasn't difficult. She'd already succeeded in turning lots of people against Anna . . . Anna Goldsmith was a cow. She was stuck-up. She was a swot. She flirted with the teachers. She thought she was better than everyone else . . . There were plenty of people who were quite happy to see her isolated.

Others were more neutral, but since we could only write down two names it wasn't hard for them to find two people that they liked better than Anna.

We were in the form room. Hayley kept moving about and getting in huddles with people and whispering. "You will put me down, won't you Ruth?" I heard her say to one girl. Ruth Smith smiled haplessly and wrote down Hayley's name.

There's a boy in our form called Richard Price. Everyone knows he fancies Hayley Parkin. She went up to him and touched his shoulder and said, "You are going to put me down, aren't you Rich?" He blushed and shielded his piece of paper with his hand.

Hayley started tickling him and grabbing at his paper. At last, she got hold of it. He'd written down two boys names. Hayley read them out and then she pretended to cry and said, "Oh Richard! How could you? I'm devastated!"

Our form teacher, Mrs Helliwell, looked up from her marking. "What's going on, Hayley?" she said.

"Sorry Miss," said Hayley. "I was just borrowing Richard's rubber. I can't spell Goldsmith."

Anna glanced at Hayley. Hayley was smiling at her.

I went to the toilet. On the way back I had to pass

Hayley's chair. She put her foot out to stop me.

"Did you put me down?" she asked. There was an edge to her voice.

"I might have," I said.

She smiled appealingly. "I put you," she said. She showed me her paper. "Look!" She pointed. "Melanie Blackwood."

I saw my name. I was surprised, and flattered as well. A little wave of pleasure went through me.

Hayley was sitting beside Siobhan Reid. Siobhan Reid's like a tartier version of Hayley. Everything Hayley does, Siobhan copies.

Hayley leaned across the desk, and putting her mouth close to my ear, she whispered, "I wouldn't bother putting Anna down. She's only using you."

As she spoke she winked at Siobhan, who pulled a piece of chewing gum from between her lips and wound it round her pen.

"You wait," said Hayley, eyeballing me. "Anna will dump you soon. Like she dumped me."

I went back to my seat. Anna was looking out of the window. I don't know what made me do it. My heart was racing. Quickly, I crossed out Anna Goldsmith and in her place I wrote Hayley Parkin.

6

Frances Goldsmith flings open the bathroom door. She feels herself freeze, as though someone has clamped her insides in ice. The screwdriver drops to the floor with a thud. She hears a strangled whimper come from her mouth.

Anna is lying on the floor with her knees crooked to her chest, like a foetus. She is motionless. Her skin has a pearly sheen like the inside of a shell.

"*Anna!*"

Frances Goldsmith goes into crisis mode, moving fast, adrenalin-driven. She kneels on the floor and shakes Anna's shoulders.

"Anna!" Her voice is urgent. "*Anna!*" She shakes her more vigorously and slaps her face with the palm of her hand. Anna rolls to one side, her head lolling like a puppet with the strings cut. Her mouth falls open like a fish. She is barely breathing.

"Don't do this to me, Anna!" Mrs Goldsmith murmurs, as she grips her daughter's wrist, searching for a pulse. She feels movement, a frantic crazy rhythm, racing and jumpy. Thank God! *Thank God!*

She prises away the blue notebook that Anna is clasping to her chest and rolls her into the recovery position. She draws Anna's hair off her face and coils it at the nape of her neck. She runs her finger round the inside of Anna's mouth. No blockages, no restrictions. Then her eyes flick round the bathroom, taking in details.

A vodka bottle on the side of the bath – all but empty.

A medicine bottle on the bath mat with the cap unscrewed. She shakes it. Empty.

A fountain pen with no lid, ink seeping out on to a towel.

Three letters, neatly folded on the bathroom chair. Frances glances at the names. Melanie Blackwood. Hayley Parkin. Mum and Dad.

She runs to the phone and dials for an ambulance. Her voice cracks as she speaks.

The wait seems endless. Frances Goldsmith paces the upstairs landing. She looks out of the window. The garden is gloomy and wet. She touches the curtains.

She tries to ring David but the hospital switchboard is engaged.

She squats on the bathroom floor, fiddling with Anna's hair, checking her pulse, willing her to keep breathing.

She goes to the bedroom and takes a bag from the cupboard. Then she runs about the house, stuffing things into it. A nightshirt for Anna. Toilet things. Paper tissues. Her make-up wallet. Her purse. The address book from the drawer in the hall. Clean underwear. A towel. Her mobile phone.

She is back in the bathroom. She picks up Anna's notebook and the three letters and drops them into the bag as well.

Anna is lying on a folded bath towel. She has surrounded it with cushions from her bedroom, like a nest. Frances picks up an orange cushion and holds it to herself. She feels her shoulders shaking.

The doorbell rings. Frances drops the cushion and runs downstairs. She cannot speak. She gestures to the stairs.

They roll Anna on to a stretcher, checking her pulse, listening to her breathing. They pinch her ear and her arm.

"No response," says one of the paramedics. He picks up the medicine bottle. "How many were in it?" he asks. He looks at the label.

Frances Goldsmith shrugs. She cannot think. "Most of them. It was a fairly new bottle. Ten, maybe? Perhaps twelve?"

"And the vodka?"

"I can't remember. There was quite a bit, I think."

"She was lucky she didn't throw up. She could have died choking on it."

The paramedics are going downstairs, carrying

Anna carefully as though she were a piano or a piece of furniture.

"Does she drink on a regular basis?" one of them asks. Frances Goldsmith opens her mouth to protest.

"No!" she says. "She doesn't drink at all . . ." Her voice trails off. What does she know? What does she know about Anna Goldsmith? What does she know about anything?

They ride in the ambulance with the blue light flashing. Frances does not speak. One of the ambulance crew puts a blanket around her shoulders. She fingers the buttons on her blouse.

7

Anna started going out with Nick in the summer holidays. She was fourteen. He was seventeen.

Nick's a friend of Tom's – one of the pop tart brigade. He's got luscious dark hair and drop-dead gorgeous eyes and everyone fancies him.

He asked her out three days before she went to France. They'd been at the park, playing tennis. They were playing doubles. Anna and Nick versus Tom and Sarah, a girl in the Sixth Form. Anna and Nick had won, three sets to love. She was wearing cycling shorts and a big white T-shirt with a cartoon jellyfish on the front. It was hot. She had to keep flapping her shirt to cool herself down. She had her hair tied back in a scrunchy and sports bands on her wrists. Nick had rivers of sweat running down the back of his shirt.

Tom invited everyone back for pizza.

"You go on!" Nick said. "I'll catch you up in a minute. I need a drink. Can I buy you a can of something, Anna?"

They watched Tom and Sarah go out through the park gates. Nick smiled at her.

"You're really good," he said.

"Thanks," said Anna.

They went to the corner shop. He bought her a Diet Coke. His fingers brushed against Anna's hand as he passed it to her.

They walked home slowly. Nick seemed to be stalling for time. They chatted about tennis and France and Tom.

As they reached the Goldsmiths' front gate Nick said, "Anna, will you go out with me?"

They stopped walking and looked at each other. Anna felt herself swallow hard. She nodded. Nick grinned. Then he slid the scrunchy out of her hair so that her hair tumbled on to her shoulders.

"You've got great hair," he said. He touched her cheek.

They sat next to each other eating pizza. Nick pressed his toe against hers under the kitchen table. He stayed late, until it was getting dark.

"Hadn't one of us better walk Sarah home?" Nick said. "It's nearly dark. Tom, could you . . . ?" Nick had winked at Tom. Tom was slow on the uptake. "Couldn't you . . . ? Sarah's is on your way home . . ."

Sarah stood up. "Come on Tom," she said. "I think someone is trying to get rid of us!"

They went, leaving Anna and Nick staring at a plate of pizza crusts. The house was quiet. Outside the kitchen window there was an indigo gleam.

"Hi," Nick said, shyly. He touched Anna's hair. And then he kissed her. His lips were really soft.

Anna felt as if she would dissolve into a pool on the floor. It was the first time she'd been kissed like that. The kiss seemed to go on for ever. Anna closed her eyes and moved her lips softly.

At last Nick pulled away and said, "God, Anna. You're so beautiful!"

I know all this because Anna told me everything in microscopic detail the next morning, sat in our back garden. She had a huge grin plastered all over her face. I was suitably impressed. I said all the right things.

"He didn't!" I said. "God, Anna! What did you say? . . . You're kidding! . . . No! Really? . . . He really said that?"

Anna told me and told me again. I could have reconstructed the scene to the absolute second!

I was happy for her. She looked all sparkly, as though the sun was coming out of her ears. She is beautiful. She has got great hair.

I was jealous too. Who wouldn't have been? Nick is fantastic. And he's a Sixth Former!

I didn't see Anna again before she went to France. I know exactly what she was doing though because she called me on the phone three times and told me.

She went to the cinema with Nick to see a Jim Carrey film, but she couldn't remember much about the film because Nick was kissing her so much. Then they went to MacDonalds and he bought her a strawberry shake and fries. After that they walked all the way home and sat on the swings in the park and held hands and Nick said he'd miss her when she went to France.

The next day they went down town and looked at CDs in WH Smith's. He bought her a CD and a silver ring from the market. When they got home he stayed to lunch and was nice to her mum. Then her mum went out – how convenient – and they lay on Anna's bedroom floor listening to CDs all afternoon.

It was after nine when Anna phoned. Nick had just left. Her lips were tingling from being kissed so much. She was in a fog, floating in the clouds, high as a kite.

I told her about my day. How I'd cleaned out the guinea pigs and mended their run. How I'd been shopping with my mum and bought a new skirt for school. How I'd played Scalextric with my little brother and watched *You've Been Framed*!!! What a sad life!

Anna was in France for three weeks. She sent me a postcard:

Dear Mel,
Weather is brill. Great tan coming on. Am missing

Nick *so much*! Can't wait to see him again.
French boys not a patch on *Nick*!!!!
Hope you're having a fab summer.
Love Anna xxxxxxx

8

Anna is on a trolley in a cubicle in Casualty. The curtains have green swirls on them. She looks as if she is asleep, deeply asleep. Nurses shine lights into her eyes and check her pulse and take her temperature. They stick leads on to her chest with tiny paper stickers to monitor her heart. A doctor clips a wire on to her finger and numbers flash on to a screen. They write on clipboards, asking Anna's mother the same questions over and over:

"Do you know exactly what she took?" . . . "How many exactly?" . . . "Do you know what time she took them?" . . . "Does she have any history of medical problems?" . . . "Does she have any allergies?" . . . "Is there any family history of heart failure, thrombosis, diabetes, liver problems?" . . . "Has she done anything like this before?" . . .

Mrs Goldsmith becomes less convinced of her answers each time she gives them. Her head is spinning. She rubs her eyes and pinches the bridge of her nose.

She speaks to a nurse. "Would it be possible to bleep my husband? David Goldsmith. He should still be here."

The nurse looks blank. Then she says, "Does he work here?"

"He's a doctor . . . an anaesthetist." Mrs Goldsmith's voice sounds snappy and impatient. She does not mean it to.

The nurse disappears and there are whispers on the other side of the curtain.

There is a pause. Then another nurse comes in. She takes Anna's temperature and looks at the cardiac monitor.

"Did they bleep him?"

The nurse looks up.

"My husband?"

"I'll just check, love," says the nurse. She smiles brightly. There is another pause and then the nurse comes back.

"Mr Goldsmith is in theatre," she says, "they've had an emergency plastic surgery case."

"Thanks," says Frances, weakly. She feels suddenly sick.

A doctor swishes in through the curtains, a different doctor from the previous one. "I think we are going to pump your daughter's stomach," he says.

He has a strong accent – Eastern European, Polish maybe. Frances Goldsmith has to strain to make out what he says.

He continues, "Because we are not sure of the dosage, or of how long it is since she took them. To be on the safe side."

"The sleeping – is that . . . ?" Frances Goldsmith isn't sure what she wants to say. She wants to know if Anna is in a coma, if she is unconscious. She wants to know if she will wake up.

"She is in a coma, Mrs Goldsmith. The antidepressants have a sedative effect but most of the coma is the alcohol," says the doctor. "She's drunk. Your daughter is very drunk." He smiles. Mrs Goldsmith does not smile back.

"So will she be all right?" She hardly dares ask.

"The drug she has taken can interfere with the rhythm of her heart. We will need to watch her closely for at least forty-eight hours with the ECG – the heart monitor. After the stomach wash she'll go down to Intensive Care."

He hasn't answered her question.

They wheel Anna to another room.

"We're just waiting for an anaesthetist," says the nurse. "They need to intubate her before the stomach wash."

"What's that?" says Frances. She wishes she had more medical knowledge. She is out of her depth.

"He'll put a tube into her airways. It's so the vomit doesn't go into her lungs. She can't gag at the moment you see because her protective reflexes are suppressed."

"Oh," says Frances.

"You may want to leave," says the nurse. She puts a large bucket beside the bed. "This isn't very pleasant."

Frances Goldsmith sits on a chair beside the door. "It's OK, I'll stay," she says.

It's the least I can do, she thinks.

9

Anna ended up in our form after all – eventually. When the lists went up before the summer holidays, Anna was in 10R – Mr Robinson's form. I was in 10S (Miss Searle). So was Hayley. So was Siobhan. So was Ruth. So was Joshua. So were most of the people Hayley hung out with.

Anna went to see the Head of Lower School – Mr Atkinson, the French teacher – to find out why she wasn't with her friends.

Mr Atkinson looked at the paperwork. "Who did you want to be with, Anna?" he asked.

"Melanie," she said. "Melanie Blackwood. I nominated her – and Hayley Parkin."

He rustled papers, checking and re-checking and then, looking embarrassed, he said, "I'm sorry, Anna. There must have been a mistake. Neither of those girls named you on their sheets."

Anna was in tears in the cloakroom. I asked her what was wrong.

"Why didn't you want me in your form?"

I felt myself go red all over. Out of the corner of my eye I could see Hayley Parkin stuffing her Kappa jacket into her locker. She came over.

"What's wrong, Anna?" she said. She touched Anna's arm.

"Get lost, Hayley," snapped Anna, pulling her arm away.

"Ooh, temper, temper," said Hayley.

"Just leave her," I said. It was the first time I'd ever stood up to Hayley Parkin. She walked away.

I lied to Anna. I said I'd put her name first on my list and that they must have muddled the papers up. It was what I wished I'd done so it was partly true.

Anna believed me. Mr Atkinson moved her into 10S. I thought she was going to kiss him when he told her. That would have made his day!

Hayley pretended to be pleased. "I don't know why they bother giving us those pieces of paper," she said, on the first day back. "They just ignore what we put anyway." She caught my eye. "I wrote your name down, Anna," she said, "even if Melanie didn't."

I glared at her.

Anna looked at me rather uncertainly. "Melanie did put my name down actually, Hayley," she said. She was trying to sound tough but it didn't quite work.

Hayley raised her eyebrows and sucked her teeth. She looks like her mother when she does that.

10

Anna and Nick split up on New Year's Eve.

There was a party at the Goldsmiths' house. Anna's dad was wearing a flashing bow tie and drinking lots of whisky. They'd rolled back the carpet in the sitting-room and Mrs Goldsmith and her friends were dancing to oldtime jazz in their stockinged feet. There was a big bowl of punch on the kitchen table with bits of oranges and apples floating on the top and lots of nice nibbly things in the dining-room. Tom's room was the disco – it's bigger than Anna's and the ceiling isn't so low. He'd moved out most of the furniture and put coloured bulbs in the lights. Blur and Travis were blasting out of the CD player. Anna's room was for talking and sitting around in. She'd lit joss sticks and candles and turned the lights down low.

I was a bit surprised that Anna had invited me to the party. We hadn't seen so much of each other since the summer. Since she started going out with Nick, in fact. Hayley on the other hand had never been more friendly. It didn't dawn on me that she was only being friends with me to get at Anna. I was stupid enough to think she liked me.

* * *

Hayley was at my house the day Anna phoned.

"It's for you!" Mum shouted. "It's Anna!"

I ran down to the hall to answer the phone. Hayley was lying on my bed when I went back upstairs.

"D' you want some crisps?" I said.

"What did she want?" Hayley asked.

"Who?" I said, playing dumb.

"Anna," Hayley said. "Why are you smiling so much? What did she say?"

"Not much," I said. "You were in the middle of telling me something about Siobhan . . . ?" I was trying to distract her.

"You're lying," she said, smiling. "I can tell."

"She just wanted a chat," I said, throwing Hayley a bag of crisps.

"Was Nick busy?" There was a catty edge to her voice.

I didn't answer.

Hayley threw a teddy at me. "You're lying Melanie. It was more than that. Let me guess. She's getting married and she wants you to be her bridesmaid!"

"No!" I said laughing.

"She's moving back down south again . . . No, sorry, that would make you sad, wouldn't it? . . . I know! She's having a party!"

I said nothing. Hayley was grinning.

"That's it, isn't it? She's having a party – on New Year's Eve."

"How did you—?"

"I'm right!" said Hayley. "I'm right, aren't I? The Goldsmiths always have a New Year's Eve party. Anna told me that once." Hayley said "Goldsmiths" in a really sarcastic voice. "Well that's nice," she continued. "I'm surprised she's invited you though, Melanie. I thought she only hung out with Sixth Formers these days."

I felt awkward. I don't like it when Hayley criticises Anna. And I knew what was coming next.

"Will you ask her to invite me as well? As a favour, Mel. She'd do it for you . . ."

"I'll mention it to her," I said. But I knew I wouldn't.

"Angus might be there!" said Hayley suddenly.

I had been thinking the same thing. I could feel myself blushing.

"Shame he's so small, Mel. He'd only come up to your armpits! Don't you think he's a bit of a weed?"

"He's not a weed," I said. I felt annoyed with her. "He's just a late developer. And he's not that small . . ."

"You'd never guess he was in the Sixth Form," said Hayley.

I wished I hadn't told her I fancied him.

* * *

Angus is a friend of Anna's brother, Tom. They're in the athletics team together. Angus is a long distance runner. He runs miles every day. He plays the clarinet too. I see him at orchestra and at wind band on Saturday mornings. He's got a yummy smile.

So there I was at the Goldsmiths' party. I was in the dining-room grazing on bits of vol-au-vent and grapes. Angus *was* there. He was in Tom's room, dancing himself into a sweat. I was trying to summon up courage to go and join him. I had cut the corner off a slab of cheese and was nibbling it when Anna came in. She looked fantastic. She had her new black dress on – velvet with ribbon shoulder straps. Her hair was loose on her shoulders. She didn't look very happy.

"Where's Nick?" she asked.

I hadn't seen him. I'd assumed he was tangled on a cushion with Anna somewhere. My mum used to say Anna and Nick looked like they'd been surgically attached to each other, like Siamese twins. They were always wrapped around each other – in the street, in the park, on the bus, in the corridors at school.

"They make you sick," said Hayley once when we were in the form room.

Anna and Nick were outside in the corridor,

kissing against the wall. It was just before lunch. Anna came in to get her bag.

"I'm surprised you need any lunch, Anna." Hayley spoke without looking up. "The way you were eating Nick!" She laughed.

Anna ignored her. She ignored everyone that term. Everyone except Nick.

"She's a bit young to be so absorbed," my mum said. My mum knows Nick's mum. They play badminton together. Mum tells me the gossip. Nick's mum thought Nick was getting too engrossed. She was worried that he'd get distracted from his A Levels and mess up. She thinks Anna's a bit intense.

"Anna's very mature," I said.

My mum raised her eyebrows. "Well, I hope she's using something!" she said.

My mum works as a receptionist at the doctor's surgery. She brings home leaflets and puts them on my bed. She goes mad about girls my age getting pregnant. "There's no excuse for it these days," she says. "You kids have so much information about everything!"

I could hear music blasting down from Tom's bedroom. Anna picked up a grape.

"Is he dancing?" I asked helpfully.

"He seems to be avoiding me," she said. "He's been funny all night."

I was thinking about Angus, wondering if there was any chance at all of me getting off with him.

"Perhaps he's in the loo," I said. Anna dipped her finger in the trifle.

Anna's dad appeared. He's very tall – six foot three maybe – and sporty-looking. He plays squash and skis a lot and walks up mountains. He wrapped his arms around Anna's shoulders from behind and kissed the top of her head.

"How's my beautiful girl?" he said. He looked mildly drunk.

Anna wriggled free. "Dad! Get off!" she said indignantly. She stomped off to the kitchen.

Anna's dad pulled a face at me.

"She's lost Nick," I said.

"Oh!" said David, with mock gravity. Then he added, "Not permanently, I hope."

I'd never thought about the fact that they might split up. They were an item, together, welded as one. Hayley reckoned it wouldn't last, but she was just jealous. It seemed to be lasting so far – a whole school term and the best part of the Christmas holidays. Anna had bought Nick a shirt for Christmas – I'd noticed that he wasn't wearing it. He'd bought her some perfume. She was wearing that – lashings of it.

Nick walked in. He helped himself to a triangle of pizza and a handful of Hula-Hoops.

"Anna's looking for you," I said. "She thinks

you're avoiding her." Nick pulled a face and took a bite of pizza.

I went into the kitchen and poured a glass of cider. Perhaps if I got drunk I could throw myself at Angus.

Anna's parents were jiving in the sitting-room. Tom came in and rifled through the fridge for a beer. He saw his parents through the open door. "Oh, God," he said. "Dad's letting go!" He laughed and went back upstairs. I followed him, cider in hand.

I bumped into Anna coming out of the loo. She'd touched up her lipstick.

"Nick was in the dining-room a moment ago," I said.

She ran past me down the stairs. It was the first time in weeks that I'd felt sorry for her.

I glanced in at Tom's room. There wasn't much space. Angus was still dancing. His hair was glistening wet. I hovered in the doorway. *Just go for it!* I told myself. *Just walk in and start dancing!*

I didn't. I went to Anna's room and sat down on a cushion with my cider. All around me couples were writhing in the shadows.

It was nearly midnight. Anna's dad had switched on the TV set. "Big Ben time!" he was shouting. "Nearly time! Fill your glasses!"

In the sitting-room the crumblies were linking hands, getting ready to sing Auld Lang Syne. I went to the kitchen for more cider. Anna's mum danced past me with a bunch of mistletoe in her hand.

The kitchen was crowded. I could hear Big Ben chiming twelve. People shouted, "Happy New Year!" Everyone was kissing everyone else.

Angus was by the fridge. He was facing me. His T-shirt said: Just do it! It was a sign! I grabbed a skinny bit of mistletoe off the kitchen table and went towards him.

"Happy New Year, Angus!" I said, rather loudly. I kissed him, right on the mouth. As I leaned towards him, I trod on his toe and wobbled, and he had to grab me to stop me landing in the drinks. It wasn't the most tidy kiss, but I'd done it – and he didn't seem to mind.

Someone grasped my arm. I turned round. Anna was staring at me. Her eye make-up was all streaked.

"Mel!" she said. "Nick's gone!"

We went upstairs. Anna's parents' bedroom was the only room we could find with no people in it. We sat on the floor behind the door. Anna sobbed like a baby. I put my arm round her shoulder and handed her tissues.

"He's finished with me," she sobbed. "He's dumped me!"

"Why?" I said. Why would anyone not want to go out with Anna Goldsmith?

"I don't know! He wouldn't say. He just said, 'I

think we should see less of each other, Anna.' *Oh, Mel . . ."*

She sobbed again. Slimy wet strands dangled from her nose.

"You're dribbling," I said. She almost laughed. I hugged her hard.

"Oh, Mel . . ." She sniffed loudly. ". . . I'm really glad you're here . . ." She laid her head on my arm. I stroked her hair.

Does it sound terrible to say I was glad? I was glad. Why did I feel so relieved? Was it because she needed me? Or was it because she was mine again – *my* friend, *my* Anna Goldsmith? I felt suddenly warm and happy. I thought of Angus downstairs and wondered if he was missing me . . .

11

The anaesthetist has his back to Frances Goldsmith. She can see needles and tubes and something that looks like a balloon. She cannot quite see what he is doing.

Frances wonders what Anna is thinking. If she has any idea what they are doing to her.

The nurse begins to feed a tube down Anna's throat. It is a fat tube, wider than a hosepipe. Anna moves slightly, twitching her legs. The nurse rolls Anna to one side so that her head is down. Anna's legs shake wildly. Then she is still again.

The nurse mixes black powder in a jug of water and begins to pour it into the top of the tube. Anna's mother watches it slosh and bubble. There seems to be gallons of it, sluicing down Anna's throat. She fills another jug and goes on pouring.

Then it starts to come. Putrid slush, gushing from the tube, syphoning into the bucket.

Frances Goldsmith looks away and covers her mouth. There is a terrible smell of vomit. She tries to look at Anna but it makes her nauseous. She closes her eyes.

The nurse holds the tube. She is hard-faced. She

does not flinch. The stuff keeps coming, gurgling more slowly now.

When we went back to school in January Anna let everyone think that *she* had dumped Nick.

"We're just friends," she said. "It was getting too heavy. We decided to cool things down a bit."

People believed her. They admired her too. Going out with a Sixth Former was cool enough, but *dumping* him too . . .

Hayley wasn't convinced. She pumped me for details. "What really happened, Mel?" she asked. "Did *he* dump *her*? Oh, come on, she must have told *you*!"

I liked being the one that knew the truth. I liked being the one Anna had trusted. I said nothing to Hayley. Nothing at all.

Hayley was mad. She started picking fault with me. "I see you've got new shoes, Melanie," she said one day in the form room. Everyone looked at my feet. "They're just like mine," said Hayley. "Did you have to copy, Melanie?"

Another day, in PE, she said, "Mel, I've got some of that Clearasil stuff. Do you want to borrow it?" I had a spot on my nose, a hard shiny one. I retaliated.

"Keep it!" I said. "I would have thought you'd need it yourself."

I sounded silly. No one laughed. Hayley's got perfect skin. Everyone can see that.

That weekend, Hayley invited me round to her house. I should have smelt a rat. Normally I was only invited round if Siobhan or Ruth were unavailable. I definitely wasn't the first choice friend. I was stupid not to realise that.

Hayley was in a really good mood. She was talking a lot. We were on the sunbed. I was lying there, naked with goggles on. Suddenly, out of the blue Hayley said, "Did Anna and Nick sleep together, Melanie?"

I was caught off guard. I should have said nothing.

"I don't think so," I said. "Not all the way, I don't think Anna—"

Hayley interrupted. "Didn't she tell you then. I'm surprised. I thought you were really close . . ."

Anna hadn't told me either way. I hadn't asked. At the beginning, when she first came back from France, when it was first getting beyond snogging, she'd told me everything. How he'd touched her boobs, how he'd kissed her tummy, how he'd put his hand inside her jeans. But then she stopped telling me. In fact, she almost stopped phoning me.

I suppose I assumed they had. I wasn't sure I wanted to know. When Anna had been going out with Nick for a while, boys in our form started calling her a slag and a slapper and making jokes about what she would and wouldn't do. I reckon a lot of it was jealousy. The boys in our year seem so immature. Anna's a bit out of their league . . .

"You've had twenty minutes," said Hayley. "You don't want to look like a lobster!"

I sat up and put my knickers on.

"Do you think he might have finished with her because she wouldn't?" Hayley was switching off the sunbed.

I opened my mouth without thinking. "No, I think he just wanted to see less of her, so he could work for his A Levels . . ."

Hayley was straight in. "So he *did* dump *her*!" She looked triumphant.

I was fiddling with the fastener on my bra. I thought of Anna's tear-streaked face on New Year's Eve.

"You won't say anything, will you?" I said quickly. "She'd be really upset if she knew . . ." It was damage limitation. I'd said it now. The knowledge was Hayley's if she chose to use it.

Hayley smiled and passed me my clothes. "Of course I won't," she said.

I almost believed her.

"Your skin looks great," said Hayley, as I laced my

shoes. "You should come and use the sunbed more often." She smiled at me.

"Thanks," I said, basking in her approval.

12

"We'll leave the ET tube in for a few hours," says the anaesthetist. "She can go down to Intensive Care now."

He peels off his gloves. He is about to go out of the door when he recognises Anna's mother.

"Frances!" he says. He looks at Anna. "Is this . . . ?" He tries to mask his surprise.

"Our daughter, Anna," she says. Her voice is unsteady.

"Does David . . . ?"

"Not yet. He's in theatre." Frances looks at her shoes.

"I'll tell him – when he's finished," he says.

"Thanks," says Frances. "Thanks, Roger."

He is about to leave and then he hesitates and says, "I'm very sorry, Frances." He glances at Anna. "I'm very sorry."

Frances nods. *So am I*, she thinks. She does not dare say it.

Anna is in Intensive Care. Tubes and flexes dangle from her like mooring ropes. Her bed is surrounded by machinery – monitors and screens, oxygen cylinders, masks and pipes, black boxes like stacking hi-fi equipment, and so many wires.

Frances Goldsmith sits beside her on a hard chair. She fiddles with the contents of her bag. She takes out her make-up purse and unzips it. She looks at herself in the lid of her powder compact and wipes lipstick across her bottom lip. It is an automatic movement, like breathing. She checks that Anna is still breathing. It is hard to tell. Her chest moves so little. She looks still as stone and her skin is deathly pale, like white marble.

The nurses check Anna constantly. They look at their watches and read the screens. They are kind. They bring Frances a cup of tea. It has sugar in it. She drinks it without noticing.

When Frances closes her eyes, she sees Anna coiled on the bathroom floor in her nest of cushions – pearly and silent. She still cannot quite believe that her daughter is not dead.

Frances is dry-eyed. Numb with shock. She fingers the letters in her bag. Melanie Blackwood. Hayley Parkin. Mum and Dad. She takes out this last one and then puts it back. She is afraid to read, afraid of what Anna may say; of what she, Frances Goldsmith may stand accused.

She pulls out the notebook. Its cover is shiny blue – like a peacock's chest. She has always resisted reading it before, though she has often seen it under Anna's pillow and buried in her underwear drawer.

Frances feels like a trespasser. She thinks of the bathroom door, locked shut against her. She wasn't due home till after six. Anna knew that. She hadn't wanted to be found. Not until afterwards.

Frances Goldsmith opens the notebook at the first page and begins to read.

13

Monday November 28th

A new diary. A new town. A new school.
Everything is new. It snowed today. (They said
it was colder in Yorkshire!) When I opened
my curtains (hideous pink ones – Mum hasn't
finished the new ones yet!) the lawn at the back
looked so clean and white – no footprints. An
unwritten page.

School was better than I expected. I was freezing
though – the classrooms are huge and draughty
and the corridors are all painted toothpaste green
which makes it seem even colder. Must get some
gloves.

I was right about the blazer. No one else
was wearing one – none of the girls that is.
Mum will be mad when she realises she's
wasted £100.

Frances Goldsmith winces at the memory of their
argument. Anna in a fitting-room cubicle, scowling at
the mirror.

"It's gross! I look disgusting in purple!"

"It's uniform, Anna."

"I won't wear it!"

Anna's eyes are full of fire. So like David when she's angry.

"Yes, you will, Anna." She hears herself. Tight-lipped. Immovable. Head to head. The clash of wills. A daughter as stubborn and bloody-minded as herself . . .

Frances turns the page and reads on.

Sat beside a girl called Hayley. Hayley Parkin – nice name. I don't know any Hayleys. She was very friendly. She said she'd look after me. I was glad. The school is like a rabbit warren. Staircases all over the place and identical mint green corridors. Hayley let me share her locker.

Maths was boring. The work was all stuff I've done before and we worked from a text book for most of the lesson. French was quite good. Nice teacher – Mr Atkinson. Quite young. Brown eyes. He used to live in La Rochelle. Told him we visited there on the way to the Gironde. La Gironde.

Had lunch with Hayley. Brown mince and rubbery Yorkshire pud. Talked about fathers – hers runs his own company, something to do with water treatment. She says he drives a Jag. Hayley didn't know what an anaesthetist was. When I told her, she asked if I'd seen Coma. *Her mum runs a sunbed rental business. Hayley says I can go over and use a sunbed. Sounds good. Mum won't like it though. She's paranoid about melanoma since she had that mole cut out.*

Frances moves her hand unconsciously to the side of her neck and traces the tiny silky scar with her fingertips. She reads on.

Double English after lunch. War poets – Wilfred Owen and Siegfried Sassoon. Homework exercise: You are in a First World War trench on the edge of the Somme. Write a letter home. (Include details of sights, sounds, smells etc . . .)

Hayley bought me a Boost bar at lunchtime. There's a sweet shop on the corner by the school gates. I asked Hayley about orchestra but she isn't musical. She says Mr Brigg, the Head of Music, is a dweeb!

Tuesday November 29th

Nice day. Double Geography, RE, French, lunch, double English then PE. We're allowed to wear cycling shorts under our gym skirts – hooray, no more wobbly white thighs! We played hockey. I scored a goal. Hayley's in the team. She says they have practice tomorrow lunchtime. It was cold on the pitch. My hands went blue!

Tom likes the Sixth Form. There are some hunky lads in his English group. I said he should invite them round! Hayley's invited me to her house at the weekend. She lives on the hill above the hospital. She says her dad will collect me. She wrote my phone number on her hand.

Mum bit my head off when I asked her about finishing my curtains. She said they were the least of her priorities. Charming! She says her school is a dump and the French department is a shambles. I said we should get a cat. Cats are good for stress. Stroking them lowers your pulse rate. Perhaps I'll ask Dad – if I can get him to listen to me for long enough!

Wednesday November 30th

Another brill day! I feel really at home already, thanks to Hayley. She's so nice to me. She bought me a Coke at lunchtime from the machine. She's very generous! I asked for a Diet Coke but there weren't any. Hayley said, "You don't need to drink Diet Coke. You've got a brilliant figure!" Hayley's much thinner than me, and a bit taller too. She's got great legs. Tom thinks she's good-looking. He says she's got nice hair. I wonder if she likes him.

Hockey was good. I played Centre Forward. I can do a team trial next Monday. Hayley says I'm better than most of the team anyway.

Mr Atkinson says my pronunciation is perfect.

He says I could pass for a French person. Mum will be pleased about that. All that coaching in French supermarkets. Nous allons acheter des croissants!

Mum says she'll finish my curtains at the weekend if I go to Sainsbury's with her and tidy my room. There's nothing in my room to tidy since we only moved in last week! Everything is still where I put it when I unpacked the boxes. Some of the boxes are still packed up in the spare bedroom but I haven't missed anything important. I think I can live without my Barbie dolls for the time being!

Wrote to Fenella and told her how much I like it here.

Thursday December 1st

Orchestra tonight. Mr Brigg said they were a bit top heavy with violins but then I told him I'd passed Grade Five with distinction and he looked impressed.

Hayley says her parents are taking us bowling at the weekend and I can sleep over on Saturday if I want. I'm not sure what Mum will say. She's always funny when she hasn't met people's parents. I think she likes to vet them to make sure they're suitable. There's always something wrong with them.

I got an A+ for my war poets homework. Mrs Mullen said my writing showed "great sensitivity" and that I had a "remarkable gift for empathy". Get that!

I asked Dad about a cat and he said maybe.

Friday December 2nd

The end of my first week. Twenty-three days until Christmas.

Had a letter from Fenella. She said she's missing me. I'm not missing her as much as I expected to. I feel lucky that I've made a new friend so quickly. Hayley linked arms with me in the corridor on the way to Maths. She said, "I'm really glad you've come to this school, Anna." She seems to like me so much. She says she loves my hair, and the way I talk.

Mum seemed more relaxed tonight. She said she was relieved to have got through the first week.

Dad says we can have a cat if I look after it. Tom says it's not fair because they wouldn't let him have a gerbil when he was eight! He was joking of course, but not totally. Tom thinks I get my own way more than he does. Sometimes I think he doesn't like me much.

I don't know what to wear to go to Hayley's. I could wear my jeans but they make my bum look big. Hayley dresses well. She even manages to look good in her school uniform which is really saying something. I could wear my silky blouse but I don't want to look overdressed. Ho-hum – as Pooh Bear would say!

Anna twitches slightly, like somebody dreaming. Frances Goldsmith looks up anxiously. She shuts the notebook like a guilty child. Caught in the act. Intruder! Nosey cow, as Anna once called her during an argument.

"Why does she do that?" Frances asks.

"They're mild convulsions," says the nurse. "That's one of the side-effects of the drug." The nurse seems unperturbed.

Anna is still again. Still and silent.

Frances opens the diary. She has lost her place. She flicks the pages, skimming. Hayley Parkin. Hayley Parkin. Hayley Parkin. The name jumps out at her.

Sunday December 4th
Slept at Hayley's. Great house. Smart bedroom. Nice parents. Went bowling – I got a strike! – and then they took us to MacDonalds. We stuffed ourselves. Just as well Mum couldn't see how much junk I ate!

Hayley gave me some earrings she doesn't want any more – silver ones. She says they suit my hair... She's so generous – and her parents are too.

Wednesday December 7th
Hayley's got some new Kickers. I wonder if Mum will buy me some . . .

Monday December 12th
Hayley hadn't done her French homework so I let her copy mine . . .

Tuesday December 13th
Only ten shopping days left till Christmas. I still can't decide what to buy Hayley . . .

Saturday December 17th
Mum finally finished my curtains today. They're really bright – stripes and zig-zags and triangles. Cherokee, the fabric's called. She made some cushion covers with the leftover material. Hayley thinks they're cool. Her bedroom is all white and pastel colours – everything matching. She says she likes mine better.

Dad went skiing for a few days this week in Glen Coe. He brought me a fluffy reindeer wearing a tartan bow tie. Hayley says it's got a face like Richard Price, a boy in our form!

Frances stretches in the chair and suppresses a yawn. She is thinking about Hayley Parkin. What exactly did go wrong between her and Anna? She had never adequately accounted for it. They'd been so close, so involved. Then it just fizzled. Perhaps it was just their age. Or was it girls? Tom never seemed to get so tangled up with his friends. He just fitted in with people. Always in a crowd. No one special friend, like Anna. There was something about Hayley Parkin, though. Something Frances didn't quite trust.

"She's a spoilt kid with too much money," David had said once. He was lying in the bath with hot bubbles round his chin and his knees poking out like two wigwams.

They had discussed the Parkin parents – or rather, dismantled them, picked them to bits.

"He's a bit flash," David said. "You see his cheque book coming before you see him!"

"And she looks like a Barbie doll!"

Frances pictured herself, her foot on the side of the bath, painting her toenails coral pink.

"So does Hayley," David said, "All that fluffy blonde hair."

"At least she's got age on her side . . . and the blonde is natural!"

"Oh! Bitch! Bitch!"

David had flicked a dollop of bath foam at her. She had deserved it. Why did it give her so much satisfaction to criticise other women?

The nurse comes to check Anna's temperature. "It's high," she says. "We need to keep an eye on that."

Frances touches Anna's arm. It feels hot and feverish.

Frances looks at her watch. Eight-thirty. She suddenly remembers Sally and Mike. Rummaging in her bag she takes out her mobile phone.

"Sorry, no mobiles," says the nurse. "It interferes with the equipment."

"Of course. Sorry," says Frances. She looks helpless and confused.

"There's a payphone down the corridor," says the nurse with a smile.

14

I rang Anna's house again at about eight-thirty but I got the answerphone. I was surprised Anna wasn't there. I wondered if she was ignoring the phone to get back at me. That would have been understandable.

Anna was supposed to be sleeping over on Saturday. Mum was hassling me about sheets and making up beds and defrosting chicken portions.

"She seems to be out," I said to Mum.

"Well, she could have the courtesy to ring you back, Melanie," said Mum. Mum doesn't like Anna much. She thinks she's snooty. She thinks Mrs Goldsmith is pushy and abrasive, and Mr Goldsmith is arrogant. That's because he's a doctor. She thinks all doctors are arrogant. She says goes with the job.

15

Frances runs her eyes across the handwritten pages. Anna was always so neat, so methodical, so sorted. She looks at Anna now, her hair dishevelled, her T-shirt spattered with vomit, a tube in her nose . . . She flicks forward, skimming the pages. Christmas . . . skiing in France . . . January . . . lots of snow . . .

Saturday February 4th

New cat at last!!! She's like a ball of black wool. We're calling her Patsy because she looks a bit dippy! Tom wanted to call her Bimbo because she's got big eyes, but Mum said he couldn't! She's definitely a bit mad. She ran right up the curtains when Mum got the hoover out.

Frances smiles. Patsy had been a crazy kitten. They'd all been glad when she stopped jumping out and pouncing on them every time they came downstairs. She was fully grown now – sedate and detached.

Frances leafs through the next few pages . . .

Orchestra concert . . . Grade Six violin (distinction again) . . . 100% in a French test . . . must go on a diet . . .

Wednesday March 22nd

Hayley's parents have invited me to go to Portugal with them at Spring Bank. They've got a villa in the Algarve. Hayley says the beaches are fantastic – not to mention the Portuguese men! The villa's got its own pool. I'll have to lose some weight so I can look sexy by the poolside. Anna Goldsmith the Baywatch Babe!

Frances had forgotten the Algarve plans. They'd never come to anything. Anna and Hayley had seemed to fall out with each other soon after that. She reads on . . .

Monday April 3rd

One week left until the Easter holidays. I'm looking forward to going to France. The weather here is foul and cold. I'm sure it was never this cold in Guildford!

Hayley was a bit strange today. I hope I haven't offended her. She moved seats in Maths and sat beside Ruth Smith. She said her eyes were hurting and she couldn't see the board properly from our seat. She's never mentioned having difficulty seeing things before.

Mr Atkinson made a big fuss about my test results and said I was a joy to teach. Hayley called me a swot. I think she was joking.

Tuesday April 4th

Hayley seemed to be ignoring me today. I might have been imagining it. During English she said she had a migraine and she went to the nurse for a paracetamol. Maybe she's just feeling a bit off-colour.

I sat with her for lunch (surf burger and chips – yuck!). Tom was talking to a lad in his Geography group. He's called Nick. He's very cute. Tall, dark hair, amazing eyes, great smile. I told Hayley I fancied him. She said, "Isn't he a bit old for you, Anna?" I was surprised. Hayley always says she'd never go out with anyone younger than Lower Sixth. Nick's in the Lower Sixth. Tom says he's a good tennis player.

Wednesday April 5th

Hayley is definitely ignoring me. She was telling a joke in the form room today – something about a bread roll and a trombone. When I walked in, she stopped talking and pretended to be looking out of the window.

It was the first time I'd worn my new shoes. I asked her if she liked them.

"Can't you be more original, Anna?" she said. "They're the same as mine."

I know they're the same as hers. That's why I wanted them, just like she bought a silk scarf the same as mine when we went to Top Shop. "You've got great style, Anna," she had said. "Really distinctive." That was only three weeks ago. I can't understand why she's acting so weird!

Thursday April 6th

Hayley changed lockers today. She swapped with Richard Price so she could have the locker next to Ruth's. I didn't say anything. It felt so petty even to notice.

She didn't speak to me all day today. I asked her how her migraine was in RE and she didn't reply. I caught her looking at me a few times and when I looked up and smiled she turned away and smirked. Other people were smirking too. It was as if there was a joke at my expense but no one was telling me what was funny. Like I had my skirt tucked into my knickers at the back or something.

Perhaps I've done something stupid without realising it. I'm definitely not imagining it. Almost definitely, anyway.

Friday April 7th

Hayley was more normal again today. They're going to Center Parcs in the holidays. She was telling me about it.

"It's like a health farm," she said. "You live

in chalets in the woods and there's a great swimming pool and jacuzzis and saunas whenever you want them. Mum and I are just going to have facials and massages and hang out in the steam room."

"That sounds nice," I said. My mum would hate that. She'd think it was a waste of time!

Hayley sat with me in French and copied the answers to the listening comprehension. I pretended not to notice. I was just glad she was speaking to me again.

As we're not going to France till Wednesday and Hayley isn't going to Center Parcs till Easter Monday, I thought she might like to come clothes shopping in Leeds sometime. I want to get some new jeans and a jacket to wear in France. I asked Hayley when we were in registration. There was a whole crowd of us standing round in the form room.

Hayley was funny with me again. She said she didn't want to come. She didn't say why.

16

There is a gap in Anna's diary. A blank page. The Easter holidays. Anna must have left the diary behind when they went to France.

Frances remembers the holiday. Not one of their best. The *gite* was damp. Tom hadn't wanted to come so he was sulky all fortnight. David kept picking on him and accusing him of being morose. Anna had been moody and difficult – claiming she was missing Fenella and the Guildford crowd. Frances herself had been rather on edge, too. Ofsted was only a month away and she'd found it hard to switch off from work. And it rained *and* the car broke down on the M1 on the way home! God, what a catalogue! She shudders at the memory.

Monday April 24th

Back to school. The summer term. It was pouring with rain. I dropped my umbrella coming down the stairs from Maths and it broke. Great start!

I was hoping things would be back to normal with Hayley but she was still acting strangely. She avoided me in French. She didn't mention my postcard. Maybe it never arrived.

Perhaps it will all blow over soon. Perhaps I

should ask her if I've done something or said something that's annoyed her...

Tuesday April 25th

PE today. No more hockey. This term it's athletics or tennis. The tennis courts are crap. Tom says the nets have gone up in the park and he's going to play there. At least that's handy for after school.

Sat with Hayley in RE. I told her I had a new Robbie Williams tape and she could borrow it. She says she doesn't like him any more. She looked at Siobhan Reid as she said it and they both laughed.

The best thing about today was Tom inviting Nick round after school. I met him on the stairs as they were going up to Tom's room. He said hello to me. He's so gorgeous!

Wednesday April 26th

Hayley Parkin is a cow! She was totally ignoring me today. I asked her if I could borrow her ruler in Maths and she looked the other way. Then she needed a rubber in CDT and I offered to lend her mine. "Thanks, Anna," she said, really sarcastically. "But don't trouble yourself!" The people sitting round her all giggled.

Why am I so funny all of a sudden?

I followed her into the toilets at afternoon break. There was no one else there. She was doing her hair in the mirror.

"All right," I said. I was mad as hell. "What have I done? Why are you acting like this?"

"Like what?" said Hayley. She smiled at me as if nothing was wrong.

"Like I'm an alien or something!" I could feel myself going red.

"You said it!" she said. She took a lipstick out of her bag.

"Have I done something to annoy you?"

She didn't look at me. She just pursed her lips in the mirror.

"Anna," she said quietly, "you've done lots of things to annoy me. You're actually a very annoying person."

I didn't reply. I went into a toilet cubicle and slammed the door shut. It was all I could do not to cry.

Thursday April 27th

If Hayley Parkin is going to ignore me, I'll ignore her too. I moved seats in English and sat with Melanie Blackwood. She's in the orchestra (she plays the clarinet) and she was in the hockey team too. I don't really know her but she seems nice enough. She's quiet and she's got mousey hair. Mum would call her nondescript.

Nick came round again tonight. He and Tom

were doing some homework on the computer. They made toast in the kitchen – piles of it. I went in to make a coffee just so I could get a closer look at Nick. He was in a blue Nike T-shirt. He's got sexy arms and big hands and such lovely eyes. Yum!!!

Friday April 28th

Nick said hello to me in the corridor today. He walked by when we were lining up to go into CDT. Most of our form were there. He smiled at me. I felt like I'd go through the ceiling!

Hayley was standing near me. Suddenly she was chatting to me, just like before, as if we were still friends. "Nick seems to really like you, Anna," she said. "He's just your type, isn't he?"

I smiled. She slipped her arm into mine. I wasn't sure how to react.

"He's got lovely eyes," she said. She was watching him disappearing down the corridor. She leaned close to me so that we were almost whispering. "And lovely arms," she went on.

I'd told her ages ago that I have a thing about arms. Men's arms that is. Mr Atkinson has nice arms. When it's warm in the classroom he rolls his sleeves up.

I found myself giggling and then I said, "He's got such long fingers too!" It was a stupid thing to *say. I don't know why I said it.*

Hayley giggled and squeezed my arm. "You know what they say about men with big hands, Anna."

I blushed crimson.

Hayley sat with me in CDT. Melanie sat with us too. Hayley was rude to Melanie. We were supposed to be designing children's toys that can be made out of wood. Then next week we're making them. Melanie isn't very good at drawing.

"What's that, Melanie?" Hayley said. She held up Melanie's pad so everyone could see it and said, "Look! Melanie's making a slug! Is it a slug, Melanie, is it?"

Melanie was bright red.

"It looks like a condom!" said Siobhan Reid. She was on the next table. She grinned at Hayley and said, "A used one!" They both laughed raucously.

"It's a snail," Melanie said quietly. "I haven't drawn the shell yet."

I felt sorry for her. "That's quite a good idea," I said.

Hayley glared at me. She didn't speak to me for the rest of the lesson.

Monday May 1st

No school today. May Day. It was sunny. I played tennis with Melanie in the park. She isn't very good so it was a bit boring for me, but she's keen. I said I'll give her some coaching.

I was going to invite her back afterwards but I decided that was a bad idea. Mum is going mental over Ofsted and we're all treading on eggshells trying not to upset her. She keeps going on at Tom about working harder. "You won't sail through A Levels doing sod all, you know," she said. Mum's paranoid! She thinks Tom doesn't work hard enough just to get back at her, when actually it's just becuase he's a lazy sod. At least she can't accuse me of not working hard enough. She had a go at me about violin practice instead.

The cat knocked over a plant in the living-room – the cheese plant, the one that goes halfway up the wall. I think she was climbing it! Mum went nuclear about the mess and blamed me, since it was my idea to get a cat – so I hoovered it up. So much for Patsy reducing our domestic stress level!

Tuesday May 2nd

Hayley is giving me the silent treatment again. She didn't say a word all day.

Wednesday May 3rd

Played tennis after school with Melanie. She's making good progress. She says I'm a good teacher. When I got home Nick was there – oh no!

My hair was all sweaty and I had a red face. I dived upstairs and got changed. When I came back down, he and Tom had gone out. Damn!

I avoided Hayley today. Melanie says ignoring her is guaranteed to make her mad. Good! Silly cow!

Thursday May 4th

Hayley has changed tactics again. She was back to the sniggering and smirking treatment today. We were in the cloakroom at home time. She started taking the mickey out of the way I talk – the way I say "a" sounds. Her audience laughed. They wouldn't dare not laugh.

It doesn't seem five minutes since Hayley was telling me she loved the way I said things.

"It sounds so much nicer than Yorkshire," she said, "the way you talk." We were sitting on her bed, trying on make-up. "Say grass," she said.

I said it, like a performing dog. She'd touched my hair, hooked it behind my ears.

"Try the eyeliner," she said. "You'll look gorgeous in that."

I never wore much make-up before I met Hayley.

Friday May 5th

Hayley had a go at me for not shaving my legs.

Not directly of course. She's too subtle for that. I should have shaved them last night but I forgot. They were a bit stubbly, and it was PE. She started going on about gorillas. The sniggerers were there, glancing sideways at me and putting their hands over their mouths.

Hayley's got a thing about body hair. Once when I was on her sunbed she started going on about waxing. "You should wax your bikini line," she said.

As if! Mum says waxing is like someone ripping plasters off you!

Saturday May 6th
Melanie came round for the first time today. I decided to risk it as I knew Mum was going out shopping. She's on a short fuse at the moment. One week to go till Ofsted – tension mounting!

Melanie kept going on about my bedroom, saying how nice it is. She says hers is all pink. Gross!

It is nice, I suppose. I've got a yucca plant now on the window sill and I've hung up the moons-and-stars mobile that Fenella sent me at Christmas. I like the sloping roof and the blue paint and the view across the park.

Melanie's house is across the other side of the park. You can see her roof from my window.

She says she'll invite me for tea.

Mum came in from shopping and was all jolly and hyper. She did her best I'm-a-marvellous-laid-back-mother act and rustled up pizza and chocolate chip cookies. Melanie thought she was great. She says her mum always stays in the kitchen when her friends come round, and peeps at them round the door. Mum asked Melanie about tennis and playing the clarinet and what her parents did. Her dad sells computers. I didn't know that.

Dad came in from playing squash. He was in a good mood too. He's always in a good mood after squash. He says he imagines the squash ball is the Hospital Manager, or the nurses he doesn't like, and then he beats hell out of it. No wonder he feels better afterwards!

Sunday May 7th
Yesterday must have been a temporary domestic blip. Today Mum was back to normal, doing the woman-on-the-edge-of-a-nervous-breakdown bit. She screamed at Dad for leaving sweaty squash kit on the kitchen floor. She screamed at Tom for playing his CD player too loud when she was doing her marking. She screamed at me for using all the hot water when I had a bath. She screamed at Patsy for scratching the arm of the sofa. She

says the inspectors will rubbish the modern languages department. She says they'll be declared a "failing school".

She's been writing assessment forms at the kitchen table since eleven o'clock this morning. She didn't even make any lunch. I fixed myself a sandwich and ate half a packet of digestive biscuits. Now I feel like a bloated walrus!

I wonder if Hayley will speak to me tomorrow. It's starting to get to me.

Frances Goldsmith looks at her watch again. It is nine-thirty. She has been reading for over an hour.

She feels sick. Was she really that awful during Ofsted? It seems a long time ago now. The report hadn't been that bad in the end. She'd come out of it OK.

She wonders if Anna hates her? Do all children hate their parents? Do all parents get it wrong?

She looks at the letter in her bag. Mum and Dad. Anna's handwriting. Does Anna blame them for her unhappiness? Frances is still afraid to open it. She'll read it when David comes. When David comes . . .

Where *is* David? *Why* hasn't he come? Perhaps they didn't bleep him at all. Perhaps Roger couldn't find him, or forgot. Perhaps David is at home, waiting to go to Sally and Mike's, wondering where they both are.

The nurse is reading Anna's monitors, writing down numbers on a chart. "Are you OK, Mrs Goldsmith?" she says cheerily.

Frances nods blankly. She is cold. Her back is stiff. She hasn't eaten since one o'clock. Her head is thumping. And the numbness is subsiding – the way gums unfreeze after a filling. Now she feels a dull ache. She feels the raw awfulness of what has happened creeping up on her.

17

When people talk about bullying you think of gangs. Helpless victims. People being beaten up. Dinner money stolen, threats of violence in dark corridors. We watched videos about bullying lower down the school. The teachers reckon our school doesn't have a bullying problem. They think that by our age we've grown out of "that sort of thing".

The trouble with Hayley and Anna was it was all so discreet, so undercover, so subtle. It got bigger gradually, like a snowball gathering snow. None of us would have called it bullying. Not then.

At the start of last year, when we went back to school in January – just after Anna and Nick split up – Hayley acted like she was friends with Anna again. She was really nice to her about Nick.

"It's dead sad about you and Nick," Hayley said. "You seemed such a good couple. Both so attractive and brainy."

Anna didn't say much at first, but slowly she began to talk.

"You can tell me, Anna," Hayley said. "I know how you must feel."

Anna told Hayley odd things about Nick, about

things he'd said, places they'd been, and things about Tom and her mum.

Sometimes I wanted to warn her, to tell her not to trust Hayley – but I didn't want Anna to think I was two-faced. I was friends with Hayley too. Just for a few weeks we hung around as a threesome. We went to the cinema. We went shopping. We sat by the swings in the park. It was nice. I half-hoped Hayley had changed. That it was going to stay like this. The three of us. Friendly and uncomplicated.

But by February Hayley was picking on Anna again, niggling at her, making her look silly in front of other people. She made remarks about Anna's appearance, about the way she walked, about her hair, about the shape of her nose, her voice, the way she stood. Anna must have been really confused.

On Valentine's Day Anna got a card. She showed it to me in the form room. It had two soppy hedgehogs on it and a ring of hearts. She was convinced it was from Nick.

"It's his writing," she said. "Look!"

I read the inside. The writing was spidery, hard to make out. *Let's get together again*, it said, then there was a question mark of kisses.

"It's from Nick, I'm sure it is," she said.

Hayley walked in. From the far side of the room

she called out, "How many Valentines did you get then Anna?"

Anna didn't answer.

"Don't tell me," said Hayley. "You got one from Nick!"

Anna looked away.

"She's blushing!" Hayley said. She continued, "I thought you didn't fancy him any more Anna. I thought you wanted to spend less time with him. After all you did dump him, didn't you?" Her voice was loaded with sarcasm.

The bell went. As we left the classroom, Hayley whispered to Anna. "Did it have two hedgehogs on it, Anna, and a ring of hearts?"

Anna looked surprised.

Hayley reached into her bag. "Like this!" she said. She pulled out a card identical to Anna's. Inside was the same spidery writing. How about it, Hayley? it said. "It looks like you've got competition, Anna!" Hayley smiled her sweetest smile and walked off.

I thought Anna was going to cry so I squeezed her arm.

"Nick wouldn't do that," I said. "I bet Hayley sent the card to you herself as a sick joke. Or how would she know it was the same as hers?"

Anna persuaded me to ask Nick. We're not really supposed to go into the Sixth Form common room so I waited by the door at the end of break. Anna wouldn't come with me. She couldn't face him.

"Hayley Parkin? Are you kidding? No way!" Nick laughed. "I didn't send any Valentine cards, Melanie. Look! I know Anna's still upset. I'm sorry . . . She's great . . . but she's just a kid . . ." He shrugged and walked off.

I was late for English. Mrs Mullen told me off. I didn't tell Anna Nick called her a kid.

"Bitch!" said Anna under her breath in the dinner queue.

Hayley heard her. I saw her smile to herself.

18

The next day it was hockey training. We played a practice match for the last quarter of an hour. Anna and Hayley were on opposing sides, both at Centre Forward. I was playing Right Half, on Anna's side.

The pitch was muddy. We were slipping and sliding everywhere. Anna had the ball. She was making good progress into their half. She passed to the Left Wing and then the ball came back to her. Hayley was way out of position, in amongst the backs, chasing Anna.

There was a tackle, sticks flying everywhere. The ball was camouflaged in the mud. I was running up behind Anna. She was in amongst a bunch of players all hacking at the ground trying to make contact with the ball.

I saw Hayley bring her stick down like an axe, against Anna's ankle. Anna yelled and dropped her stick. The coach blew her whistle. Anna was clutching her foot and grimacing.

Hayley put her hand on Anna's back. "Are you all right, Anna?" she said. "I must have clipped her with my stick, Miss. I'm really sorry. Is there a bruise? Oh Anna! Sorry!"

It was a convincing performance. Everyone thought it was an accident.

19

The things Hayley did were trivial in themselves. There was nothing major. Nothing you could really prove.

She wrote things on Anna's rough book. Silly stuff. *Anna Goldsmith is a swot. Anna Goldsmith is a bitch. Anna Goldsmith loves Mr Atkinson 4 eva!* Most people ignored her, but the rest seemed to find it funny.

Then it was messages. Scruffy bits of paper handed round the class. Furtive. Childish. *Anna Goldsmith needs liposuction. Anna Goldsmith is a slag. Anna Goldsmith was dumped.*

Sometimes the notes bypassed Anna so that people giggled and smirked and she didn't know why. Like a conspiracy.

Sometimes Hayley got Siobhan to put the notes on Anna's desk or in her exercise books. Hayley always managed to hide them, to secrete them away before a teacher saw. She covered her tracks. She concealed her evidence.

Anna tried not to react. She didn't retaliate. After a while she didn't even blush. I was surprised. I thought she'd be more upset.

The messages got nastier. One day Anna opened her English book to find one scrawled across a piece of scrap paper inside. She scrunched it into a ball quickly but out of the corner of my eye I saw it. *Anna Goldsmith gave Nick Simpson a blow job.* Anna stuffed the paper into the bottom of her bag.

"What's up, Anna?" Siobhan shouted.

Hayley was walking towards her. "Isn't it true?" she said, smiling. "It's just we'd heard—"

Mrs Mullen interrupted. "Hayley, what's going on?"

Hayley didn't bat an eyelid. "I was just asking Anna about the homework, Miss," she said.

Anna looked accusingly at me. I tried to remember what I'd told Hayley. She has a way of making you part with information you'd meant to keep secret.

A few days after that there was a message in Anna's RE book. *Anna Goldsmith doesn't give blow jobs!* Anna ripped the note into bits and put it in the waste paper bin. Then she asked to go to the toilet. She was gone for ages.

Sometimes there were things written on the blackboard in the form room in the morning. Nasty, really personal things. The sort of things you see on toilet walls.

Hayley always managed to rub them off before Miss Searle arrived. Once she left it a bit late. She had the board rubber in her hand as the teacher walked in.

"What are you doing Hayley?" Miss Searle looked suspicious.

Ruth Smith laughed.

"Just cleaning the board for you, Miss," said Hayley. She put the board rubber on the shelf and dusted chalk off her hands.

"Thanks," said Miss Searle uncertainly.

Hayley grinned at everyone as she sat down.

I felt caught in the middle.

"Doesn't she make you sick?" said Siobhan. She was chewing gum.

We were in CDT. Anna was at her violin lesson. I was making a coil pot out of clay.

"She's so bloody good at everything." Siobhan tossed her hair like Anna does and pulled a face. "Such a goody two-shoes!"

I said nothing. My clay wouldn't form a sausage. It kept cracking and crumbling.

"It's too dry," said Ruth Smith. "Put some water on it."

I went to the sink and filled a jug.

When I came back Hayley said, "She only hangs round with you because she hasn't got any friends, Melanie."

"Who?" I said, pretending not to be listening.

"Don't give me who!" said Hayley. She flicked a crumb of clay across the desk at me.

I slopped some water on to my clay. It made it slippery, like soap. Brown liquid oozed through my fingers.

"Mud pies," I said, trying to change the subject. My clay had stuck to the desk in a muddy heap. I scraped at it with a knife.

"Don't you get fed up with her?" Ruth said. She coiled her clay in a neat whirl. I ignored her. She tried again. "Don't you find it patronising, all this tennis coaching and stuff?"

"Melanie just fancies Tom," said Siobhan. "She's keeping in with Anna so she can go round to the Goldsmiths' house."

I blushed. I couldn't help it.

"He is a bit tasty," said Hayley. "But he's not Melanie's type. She likes skinny orchestra nerdy guys – like Angus! It's Angus you like, isn't it Mel?"

I blushed even more. Nothing had happened since New Year's Eve. Angus acted like I didn't exist.

"I don't know how you can stand going round there," said Siobhan. "Hayley says Mrs Goldsmith's so uptight all the time. No wonder Anna's like she is . . ."

"I think Frances is nice," I said.

Hayley smiled. "Frances!" she mouthed silently, raising her eyebrows.

"She's nice to me," I said. It was true. I really like Anna's parents. Her mum is a bit hyper – always rushing around – but she's nice.

"You've got clay on your face," said Hayley. She licked her finger and rubbed at my cheek.

Siobhan was grinning at me. "You should hear what Mrs Goldsmith says about you when you're not there, Melanie!" she said.

"You should hear what Anna says!" said Ruth.

"Poor Melanie," said Hayley. "You think everyone likes you. If only you knew . . ."

"Get lost!" I said. I squeezed my clay into a ball and slapped it down on the table.

"What's wrong, Mel?" said Hayley calmly. "Can't you take a joke?"

20

Wednesday February 14th

Got a Valentine card in the post. I think it was from Hayley. The cow! She made it look as if Nick had sent it. I wish I hadn't fallen for it. I tore it up and put it in the dustbin. I wonder if Nick got mine. Mel said he didn't mention it. At least he doesn't fancy Hayley Parkin. Mel says he said, "What? That tart? No way!"

Monday March 4th

Hayley's writing messages again. It's so childish. I can't believe people find it so funny. My pencil case mysteriously disappeared in Maths. I had to borrow a pen. "Have mine," said Hayley. She threw it across the classroom so it landed on my desk. There was a piece of paper folded up and stuffed into the lid:

> Roses are red
> Violets are blue
> Anna Goldsmith's a tart
> And a fat cow!

It doesn't even rhyme! I've been thinking of writing some messages back:

> *Hayley Parkin is a slag*
> *Her dad's a prick*
> *He drives a Jag*
> *Her mum's an airhead*
> *What a hag!*
> *No wonder Hayley's such a bag!!!*

Boom! Boom! But why stoop to her level? I wouldn't debase myself. Anyway, that's what she wants. She wants me to react. She wants me to retaliate so she can say that I'm paranoid. That I'm going over the top. That I've got no sense of humour.

I'm not going to play into her hands. I'll play it cool. Let her think I don't give a shit.

Thursday March 28th

It's the stuff about Nick that really gets to me. How does she know so much? Melanie must have told her. Or maybe they're just lucky guesses. I wish my face didn't give so much away.

Melanie says I take it too seriously. They're only doing it for a laugh, she says. We'd just got off the bus from school. It was raining. We stopped to shelter under the slide in the park.

There's a kind of den underneath, built from wood with a bench to sit on. It's meant for little kids, but people from our school go there. There's loads of graffiti. We sat down on the bench. I was reading the graffiti above my head. Most of it was fairly obscene. It's just as well the kids who play there can't read. Suddenly Melanie started laughing.

"What's up?" I said.

"Look," she said, pointing.

I read it out loud. "Richard Price is well sad."

Melanie was still laughing.

"What's funny about that?" I asked.

"It's Hayley's writing," said Melanie.

"So?" I said. "Why does that make it funny?"

"Well he is," Melanie said.

"What, sad?" I said.

"Yeah, he's a nerd. He's such a creep. He really fancies Hayley and she thinks—"

Melanie didn't finish. I interrupted. "Do you laugh at the things Hayley Parkin says about me too?"

Melanie stopped laughing. She didn't answer.

"Well, do you?" I said. I looked straight at her.

"No," she said. "Of course I don't. You know I—"

"What about when I'm not there? Do you laugh then?"

"Don't be paranoid, Anna."

"Answer the question, Melanie!"

I glared at her. She stared back at me.

"No, Anna. I don't actually." She picked up her bag and stood up.

"But you don't exactly stick up for me, do you?" I said.

"Anna, it's not as if—"

"You always seem pretty keen to suck up to Hayley Parkin."

"I do not suck up to anyone!" Melanie looked mad as hell.

"What is it, Mel, are you scared of her or something?" I said.

Melanie didn't answer. She stomped off towards the swings. I grabbed my violin and followed her.

"Well, are you?" I said.

Melanie's hair was hanging in wet twists down the back of her coat. She stopped by the swings and turned to face me.

"Anna," she said. "Just drop it."

Friday March 29th

Melanie didn't speak to me in Maths. She sat with Ruth Smith.

I apologised to her at break. We were beside the lockers. "I'm sorry I got mad with you," I said. "You're right. I probably am being paranoid."

Melanie was looking away, stuffing her PE bag

into her locker. Her clarinet case slid out of the locker and clattered to the floor. I picked it up.

"Mel?" I said, handing it to her. "Truce?"

She looked at me.

"I'll be your best friend!" I said it in a silly voice, sending myself up, pretending to be seven.

Melanie smiled. She looks so nice when she smiles. She is my best friend. She's the only friend I've got.

"You've got ink on your chin," I said. I licked my finger and rubbed at it. It didn't go.

"It's permanent," she said, laughing. "I'm marked for life!"

We laughed. Out of the corner of my eye I could see Hayley Parkin watching us.

21

Saturday March 30th

Mum cooked cannelloni tonight. I didn't eat it. It was a big deal.

"What's the point in me cooking if you just push it around your plate?" she said. "I don't know why I bother! It took me hours to make this!"

"It's delicious, darling," said Dad, trying to overcompensate.

Mum ignored him. "What's wrong with it?" she asked.

"I don't like the spinach," I said.

"You haven't even tried it," said Mum. I poked it with my fork. "It's good for you," said Mum.

That's her answer to everything. Cabbage – it's good for you. Homework – it's good for you. Violin practice – it's good for you. Misery – it's good for you.

"It's got iron in it," she said. "You need iron or you'll get anaemic. You look pasty enough these days as it is!"

"Oh thanks!" I said.

"Well you're not getting anything else!" said

Mum. She clattered her knife down on her plate.

"That's fine," I said. "I'm not hungry." I didn't feel like eating anything anyway.

There was a pause. Mum stared at the tablecloth and chewed aggressively.

"It's great, Mum," said Tom. "Can I have some more?" Tom always sucks up to Mum. He thinks it will give him a quiet life. It doesn't make any difference. She still has a go at him every five minutes. He helped himself to some more and ate it enthusiastically.

"Don't chomp, Tom!" said Mum.

I took a piece of cucumber from the salad bowl and nibbled it.

"Don't use your fingers," said Mum snappily. Tom smirked. Mum looked at me. "I don't know what's got into you recently, Anna! I don't like your attitude! You don't communicate! You don't eat! You sit about the place looking tired and washed out all the time!"

"Well sorr-ee!" I said, standing up and chucking my napkin on to the table. I slammed the kitchen door.

"Leave her, Frances," I heard Dad say.

Later I heard them talking about me. I listened through the crack in the kitchen door.

"She's so surly," said Mum. "She doesn't seem herself."

How come it's taken her this long to notice?

"She's just at an awkward age," Dad said. He rubbed Mum's shoulders.

"Do you think it's Nick?" Mum said. "Is she still getting over it?"

"I expect so," said Dad. He kissed the top of her head.

Mum came up to my bedroom. I was watching telly. She sat on the bed behind me.

"You'll get over him eventually," she said. I didn't look at her.

"Who?" I said.

"Nick," she said. She touched the back of my hair. "It won't always hurt," she said. She said it in an Agony Aunt sort of voice.

"It doesn't hurt now," I said.

"You'll have plenty more boyfriends, Anna. Don't worry."

"Plenty more fish in the sea," I said. She smiled. I think that's such a crap saying but I didn't say so.

"You're still very young, Anna," she said. "I think school's more important than boyfriends at this stage, don't you?"

I smiled and pretended to agree. I suppose at least she was making the effort.

Frances Goldsmith scans the pages, trying to make sense of it all. Anna was right. She had assumed it was all the stuff with Nick that was making Anna not quite herself this time last year. Anna had moped about a lot with a pale face. And there had been all those days off school with coughs and colds and unexplained tummy pains. She remembered she hadn't been very sympathetic but it wasn't as if she could just not go to work. David hadn't been much help.

There had been that business about Hayley Parkin bullying Anna, but that was much more recently. It had seemed like a lot of fuss about nothing. A bit of a storm in a teacup. Surely all girls fell out with each other from time to time. It wasn't as if she was being punched or beaten up or forced to shoplift in Woolworths or anything.

Bullying was a much bigger problem at *her* school. They'd uncovered a drugs ring in Year Nine. Hapless thirteen-year-olds being made to part with their pocket money for scabby bits of cannabis. But at Anna's school – most of the kids were from middle class homes, nice families. And anyway, Anna could stand up for herself. She was a bright enough girl, and certainly not shy.

Frances looks at Anna now, festooned with wires. She looks at Anna's heartbeat dancing on the monitor.

Perhaps she is wrong. Perhaps Anna can't stand up for herself at all . . . Perhaps Frances Goldsmith doesn't know the first flaming thing about her daughter . . .

22

By the time the summer came, Hayley was picking on Anna all the time. It was unrelenting. Everything Anna did was wrong.

Why did Anna have to work so hard? . . . Why did Anna always know everything? . . . Why did she always have her hand up in class? . . .

Teachers made it worse without realising.

"Let's have someone apart from Anna Goldsmith answering this time please." . . . "We know Anna knows, but do *you* know the answer Joshua?" . . . "There wouldn't be a problem Year Ten, if you all worked as hard as Anna Goldsmith." . . .

Anna started putting her hand up less, pretending she didn't know answers when she did. She even botched the odd piece of homework or handed it in late – anything to seem less conspicuous.

Hayley made remarks about Anna's clothes.

"Isn't that skirt a bit tight for you Anna?" . . . "Didn't they have a jumper your size?" . . . "You look good in black Anna. It suits your moods!" . . .

Anna got a new jacket. Hayley said, "Did you decide not to get a new jacket then, Anna?"

Anna changed the way she did her eye make-up. Hayley said, "Anna looks better with less make-up, don't you think? The eyeliner's a bit tarty, Anna. You wouldn't want to give the wrong impression would you?"

Most people thought Hayley was going over the top, going too far. One day she was making a joke about the mole on Anna's chin. We were by the lockers. It was home time. "She's got a bigger one on her tummy," Hayley said. "Perhaps she's got skin cancer." No one laughed at this.

On the way home I heard Ruth Smith say to Joshua, "That was sick, what Hayley said about Anna. She's being a real cow these days!"

Siobhan Reid heard her say it. She told Hayley. The next day Hayley got Siobhan to slap Ruth's face in the cloakroom. Hayley was standing by, watching. "Just watch who you're calling a cow, Ruth!" Hayley said quietly.

There were only two weeks left of the summer term by then. Anna was going to France. We were going to Gran's cottage in Wales.

"I can't wait for the holidays," said Anna. She looked exhausted. I think Hayley's behaviour was really grinding her down. She didn't say much. She'd got much quieter, less outgoing, as if she wanted to blend into the background more. As if she wanted to become invisible.

I think Hayley must have realised she was losing friends. People laughed less at her jokes. They talked about her behind her back. Her control was slipping.

Hayley's response was pretty predictable. She started greasing up to everyone. She bought lots of sweets at lunchtime and gave them out in the form room. She paid people compliments: "That's a nice bag, Ruth." ... "I like your hair, Melanie," ... "Where did you get those earrings? I really like them." ...

She even said kind things to Anna: "You were great in the play, Anna."

Anna had the main part in the summer play, *Electra*. She was really good. She hadn't wanted to do it.

"I won't be any good," she said. "I won't be able to remember all the lines." It wasn't like Anna to think she couldn't do something.

Mr Brigg persuaded her. He told her no one else would be able to handle the part. I expected Hayley to be jealous. Anna had to wear this floaty white dress. She looked wonderful.

"That dress was fabulous," said Hayley. "You looked just like Kate Winslet!"

Anna looked confused. That was just what Hayley wanted.

We went to Wales for the first two weeks of the holidays. Anna went to France the day before we got back. She was gone a fortnight so it was a whole month before I saw her again. When she came back there were just over two weeks of holiday left.

We went on a day trip to the Yorkshire Dales. The Goldsmith family plus me, plus Angus. Anna fixed that one.

"I'll get Tom to invite Angus, Mel," she had said. She had grinned and nudged me. We were in town, looking at the make-up in Boots.

Anna was really suntanned from France. She looked great. I said so. "You look much more like you again, Anna," I said.

"That's because I haven't seen Hayley Parkin for a month," she said. She laughed as if she didn't mean it.

"Does she get to you that much?" I asked. Anna was trying on a lipstick tester, pouting to herself in a tiny mirror.

"I don't want to talk about it actually, Mel," she had said.

We walked up a hill called Pen-y-ghent. Frances took a photo of us all hanging on to the cairn at the top. It was windy. My hair was all over the place. We had a picnic and some sheep nicked my crisps.

Then we went to a river where lots of people were swimming. It was really hot and sunny. There was this waterfall that flowed into a deep black pool. Tom and Angus jumped into it, off the top of the waterfall, in their trainers and shorts. They said it was freezing.

Angus looked funny in shorts. He's got really skinny legs.

We had fish and chips on the way home. It was a really ace day. Everyone seemed so happy.

"It's nice to see you again, Mel," Anna said. "I'm glad you had a good time in Wales."

I didn't tell her about the Algarve. I was hoping no one else would tell her either. The Parkins had invited me to their villa for a week while Anna was in France. I'd never been abroad before. We always go to Wales. They had even offered to pay for my flight. It had seemed too good an opportunity to miss. The beaches had been fantastic.

23

Frances Goldsmith goes on reading.

Tuesday May 21st
I didn't do my English homework. I didn't forget. I just decided to mess up for once. Mrs Mullen went on and on about how disappointed she was. Daft cow!

Wednesday May 22nd
Mr Brigg wants me to be the lead part in the summer play. It's called Electra. *It's Greek. I said I didn't want to do it. If I'm good – which I won't be – everyone will complain that I'm showing off. "Look at her, she thinks she's so* clever!*" . . . "Who the hell does she think she is?" . . . "Teacher's pet!" . . . "Anna Suck-up Goldsmith!" If I'm useless – which is more likely – I'll get laughed at. One more thing to take the piss about . . .*

Thursday May 23rd
Must go on a diet. My bum looks enormous in my new skirt. I've got a spot on my forehead – it looks like a boil. Maybe I'm ill.

Friday May 24th

I stayed off school today. I said I had a sore throat and earache. Mum believed me. She phoned at lunch time to make sure I was OK. She had left me a salad in the fridge. I put most of it in the compost bin and ate a packet of chocolate digestives. When Mum came home I said I felt sick. I did as well.

Tuesday June 4th

I finally said yes to Electra. Mr Brigg didn't give me much choice. He said I'd be "letting him down" if I didn't do it. Mum was delighted. I suppose it can't make things much worse.

Hayley says my nose is crooked. She says my eyeliner looks wrong. I wish it didn't bother me. I wish I didn't care what she thinks.

Wednesday June 5th

Siobhan says I should use henna on my hair. She says it would liven it up a bit. Hayely says if I used treatment wax it wouldn't get so frizzy. She said I should have a trim to get rid of all the split ends. I didn't realise I had split ends. I've got another big spot on my chin.

Thursday June 6th

Rehearsal for the play at lunchtime. I've got some

really embarrassing lines and I have to kiss Richard Price. Uh oh.

Nick came round tonight to do some revision with Tom. Their A Levels have started. Tom doesn't seem very stressed out. They spent most of the time playing on Tom's Dreamcast! Nick hardly spoke to me. I felt like the invisible woman.

Tuesday June 11th
Hayley's found out about Richard Price, in the play. There was a note on the board before registration: Richard Price is Anna Goldsmith's toyboy! Ho-ho.

Monday June 17th
Today Mum hit me for the first time in years.

I was in the kitchen making toast after school. Mum came in. She slammed a pile of exercise books down on the table and filled the kettle. I was spreading peanut butter on my toast.

"I thought you were on a diet," she said. (I told her I was the other day, and she said that was stupid because I was quite thin enough. She was mad because I left half my dinner.)

"Peanut butter's good for you," I said. "It's full of protein."

"It's also full of calories," said Mum. "You'd be

far better off eating proper meals than snacking all the time."

I got a plate from the cupboard.

"Aren't you going to put the jar away?" Mum said. She started unloading the dishwasher. I sighed and screwed on the peanut butter lid.

"Have you done your violin practice?" she said. I hadn't. I said I had. She didn't believe me.

"You're not doing anything like enough practice at the moment, Anna. I'm not going to keep paying for lessons if—"

"I haven't got time!" I said. Mum hates being interrupted. She glowered at me. "It's the play," I said. "I've got all those lines to learn. And I've got coursework due in . . ."

Mum slammed the china cupboard shut. "You'll just have to be more organised!" she said. She opened the fridge and took out an uncooked chicken. It looked pale and pimply.

"I can't do everything!" I snapped.

"I *have* to *manage it!*" she shouted, thumping the chicken down on the bench. She ripped off the cellophane wrapper and stuffed it into the swing-top bin.

I licked peanut butter off my fingers and put my plate in the sink.

"If you want to be superwoman that's your problem!" I said.

Mum had her back to me. She was washing her fingers under the tap. Suddenly she spun round and slapped my face. Her hand was all wet. Cold trickles of water ran down my neck.

Tuesday June 18th

I got a B- for my French homework. The second one in two weeks. Mr Atkinson said it was a worrying trend and was I OK. I said it was the play, taking up all my time. So many lines to learn etc . . .

I got my costume today. It's like a nightie. I tried it on after school. You can see my boobs through it. They look like melons. I'll look fat on stage. I don't want to wear it. I didn't want to be in the stupid play anyway. I'm totally dreading it.

I phoned Melanie but she just went on and on about Angus. How she sat by him at the wind band concert and shared his crisps. How he bought her a Solero during the interval. Big deal!

Monday July 8th

Hayley was nice to me today. She said she's looking forward to the play. She got changed next to me in PE and smiled at me a lot. Siobhan Reid looked worried. She kept looking at me with a hard stare, making her eyes small and piggy.

It's easier when Hayley ignores me. At least

then, I know what to expect. When she's friendly I start hoping. I can hate her all the while she's cold-shouldering me. I'm like ice. I don't feel anything. Then she turns nice again and it's like being stroked. Like when you rub Patsy's ears and she forgets all about washing herself, or scratching the chair or whatever it was she was doing. She leans against your hand and purrs like a motorbike. I'm like that if Hayley smiles at me. I feel myself starting to purr. I feel myself going soft round the edges, wishing she'd like me. Wishing she'd be my friend again.

I hate myself. I'm so pathetic!

24

Saturday July 20th

Holidays at last. Dad took me to the Lake District for the day. Just me and him. I don't think Mum was too happy. We climbed a mountain called Helvellyn. It was brilliant. It took us all day. I love the feeling you get when you're going up a steep bit. You plant your feet on the rock, or a tuft of grass, looking for a foothold and you feel the muscles pulling in the back of your calves. You feel hot and out of breath, but you keep going, just a bit further – pushing yourself. Then you stop and look back at where you've just climbed and you get a dizzy, light feeling in your head.

Dad walks so fast. I had to burn it to keep up. We didn't talk much. Dad's not a great talker. He asked the odd question: Was I looking forward to France? Had I enjoyed the orchestra concert? Were my walking boots comfy? I answered yes to all of them. It was nice to have a day without talking about Hayley Parkin.

At the summit there was a small round lake. It looked like blue glass, like the blue you get in stained glass windows. Like at Chartres –

ultramarine. We could see for miles. The hills had wonderful shadows on them and different shades of green – bracken and grass and scrubby bushes down in the valleys. The sky was deep blue with a single cloud, over Ullswater, like a long white thread.

On the way down we came along a ridge called Striding Edge. It was like walking along the very top of a roof – the pointy part, like a knife edge. There were steep scree slopes either side of us.

Dad walked behind me. "Just go at a steady pace," he said. "Watch out for loose pieces of rock and don't look down!"

I walked carefully. Some of the time we had to scramble, gripping the rock with our hands.

"The weather is perfect," said Dad. "I've been over here in ice and snow and this ridge is no joke then! People die up here, if they slip."

"Thanks, Dad," I said. "That makes me feel brilliant!"

"At least you're with a doctor," Dad said, gripping my arm.

At the bottom, in Glenridding we went into a pub. Dad bought me half a pint of cider.

"You could pass for eighteen," he said. "No one will know."

"They'll think I'm your young floozy," I said. Dad laughed.

"My bit on the side!" he said.

Don't let Mum hear you say that, *I thought.*

25

David Goldsmith is walking towards Intensive Care. He walks quickly with long, loping strides. His wife hears him in the corridor outside the room.

"Anna Goldsmith!" He raises his voice. "Yes, she's my daughter, for God's sake!"

Now David is in the doorway, silhouetted by the light outside. A nurse is behind him, hovering nervously. He does not speak to Frances. He goes straight to Anna, takes her pulse, opens her eyelids, reaches for the notes. "Why isn't she on lignocaine?" he barks, glancing at the ECG.

"The doctor thought it wasn't necessary . . . there's no cardiac irregularity . . ."

"That's just as well, isn't it! Why wasn't she given a prophylactic dose?"

"She didn't need one," says the nurse rather curtly.

David scans her notes. "Who's seen her?" he asks.

"Dr Benn and Dr Rawenski in Casualty," says the nurse.

"God!" says David, interrupting under his breath. "That's all she needs."

"Dr Rawenski authorised the stomach wash," says the nurse, ignoring his remark. "Dr Hurding's seen her since she came up to ICU."

David Goldsmith is still in his theatre gown, a green mask dangling round his neck. He runs his fingers through his thick black hair. "Who intubated her?" he says.

"Roger Coldwell," says the nurse.

"And he's leaving the ET tube in?"

The nurse stares at him, expressionless. "For the time being, yes," she says. She walks to the next patient.

David slams Anna's file down on the end of the bed "*What* did she take?" he says, as though he doesn't believe the notes.

"Prothiaden and vodka," says Frances quietly. The words sound horribly familiar. They roll easily off her tongue.

"What dosage? How many?" He is impatient. His face is hostile.

"Read the notes," says Frances, wearily. "You're the doctor."

"Twelve?" says David.

"Something like that." Frances fiddles with the handles of her bag.

"Where did she get Prothiaden?" he says, shaking his head.

Frances fidgets in her chair. "I had some," she says.

He glares at her.

"I got them from the GP a few weeks ago. I've been

115

feeling . . . I wasn't sleeping . . . I didn't want to . . ."

Frances is floundering. David looks incredulous.

"Well, where the hell were they?" He is shouting. The nurse looks up. "How did Anna get them?"

Frances stares at the ECG. Tidy peaks, identical mountains, side by side, like a child's drawing.

David towers over her, all six foot three of him, looming above the chair. Frances does not look at him.

"They were in the kitchen," she says. "On the shelf . . . I didn't think—"

"God, Frances!" David pulls his mask off and throws it on the floor.

"Don't blame me!" Frances's face looks fragile, like a mask about to crack. "It's not as if Anna couldn't . . ." She doesn't finish the sentence. Her voice is drowned by sobs, coming from deep inside her, cracking in her throat.

David walks to his wife's chair. Blindly, unconsciously, she stands up so that he cradles her against his chest.

"Why did she do it, David?" Frances sobs. "Why did she want to die?" She feels as if she will drown in tears. She catches her breath.

David cups his hand around her head and presses her to himself. He does not cry. He has forgotten how to. Instead he rocks his wife and says, "God knows, darling. God knows."

26

Thursday July 25th

Still over a week until we go to France. I'm bored.

Mum is redecorating the sitting-room. She's painted it blue and now she's stencilling leaves and bunches of grapes all round the top of the walls, like a frieze. She's going to sponge-paint the fireplace so it looks mottled. She said I could help – but I'd probably do it wrong.

Mum can't stand it when I'm bored. Don't mope about! she says. She hates idleness. "Why don't you do some violin practice," she said. She was up a ladder with a scarf tied round her hair. I was in the doorway. "Mind the paint!" she said. "I've just glossed the door frame . . . It's a good chance to get on top of your exam pieces," she said.

I've got Grade Seven coming up in the autumn.

"It's too hot," I said. "My bow gets slippy."

It is hot. We're having a heat wave. The weather men are talking about a drought.

"Why don't you phone someone?" says Mum. I could tell she wanted me to go away so she could get on with her painting.

"Melanie's away," I said. "She's at the cottage in Wales."

"Well, surely Melanie's not your only friend," she said with a weary laugh.

If only she knew.

"Couldn't you ring Hayley?" she said.

"No Mum, I don't think that would be a very good idea," I said. I said it in a stroppy voice. Mum was offended.

"I was only trying to be helpful," she said. She dipped her sponge in the paint.

"Well don't go on at me all the time!" I said. I went into the garden and lay on a rug on the grass.

Friday July 26th

There's a girl two doors down called Kelly. She doesn't speak to me normally. She goes to Mum's school on the other side of town. She failed the exam to get into our school. She hangs around with a gang of kids from her school. They sit in the park under the slide and call us toffs and swots when we walk past.

Kelly was on a sun lounger on their back lawn. She was coating herself in suntan oil. I was leaning out of my bedroom window.

"Hi," I said. I didn't expect her to answer.

"Hi," she said.

"How's your tan coming along?" I asked.

"Not bad," she said. "I peel though."

She's got red hair and freckles. Her shoulders looked a bit red.

"Shouldn't you be using that high protection factor stuff?" I said.

She looked blank. Surely everyone knows about melanoma – slip-slop-slap and all that.

She didn't answer. Instead she said, "You're dead lucky, being dark. I bet you go brown really easily."

"I suppose so," I said. Hayley used to go on about my tanning potential too. I can't see what all the fuss is about. Mum says, in a few years time it will be fashionable to be pale. Everyone will be wearing total sunblock.

"Holidays are boring, aren't they?" Kelly said. She rolled her top up so that her tummy was showing.

"I'm too hot," I said. I was about to shut the window and fix a drink but then on the spur of the moment I said, "Do you fancy going across to the park?"

We sat on the grass under the trees. Kelly started making a daisy-chain.

"What's my mum like as a teacher?" I said. "Is she a cow?"

"She's OK," said Kelly, "But everyone hates French anyway."

I laughed as if I hated French too.

Kelly looked at me and said, "I bet you're really good at French aren't you?"

I thought of Mr Atkinson: "Magnifique, Anna. Très bon!"

"I'm all right," I said.

"What's it like at your school?" Kelly said. "Is everyone dead brainy?"

"Nah," I said. "No one works that hard. Most people hardly ever go in the library." I do. I get the mickey taken for it: Bookworm. Superbrain. Swotty cow!

"Those blazers are disgusting," said Kelly.

"No one wears them," I said. "They're not compulsory." Compulsory. That was a stupid swotty-sounding word to choose wasn't it?

"The boys do," said Kelly. "They look a right bunch of tossers!"

I laughed so she'd think I agreed.

I slid a blade of grass between my thumbs and blew to make it squeak. It hooted like a clarinet.

"How d'you do that?" Kelly said. She laid her daisy-chain across her knee.

I started showing her, explaining how you need a wide blade, how you make a space at the base of your thumbs, how you can alter the note by

121

squeezing the grass more tightly. I stopped because I didn't want to sound like a know-all.

Kelly couldn't do it. "It doesn't work," she said.

"It takes lots of practice," I said.

She dropped her piece of grass and went back to her daisy-chain. I started making one too, splitting the fat stalks with my thumb nail.

Suddenly she laughed and said, "Your cat crapped in my mum's flowers. She was dead mad!"

27

Monday July 29th

I knocked on Kelly's door today to see if she wanted to come into town with me. It was grey and cloudy. The heat wave seems to have gone. Kelly's mum answered the door. She looked at me as if I was a lump of dog muck on the pavement.

"Kelly's out, I'm afraid," she said coldly.

"When will she be back?" I asked.

"I don't know," she said. She was already shutting the door.

I walked back down the path and along to our gate. As I turned to go into our house I looked up at Kelly's bedroom window. There was Kelly looking out through the net curtains, fiddling with her hair.

Wednesday July 31st

I persuaded Tom to play tennis with me in the park. "It'll have to be in the afternoon," he said. He doesn't get up till lunchtime since his exams finished. Mum goes mad with him.

We walked past the swings on the way to the courts. Kelly was sitting on a bench by the see-

saw with some lads from her school.

"Hi!" I shouted. I waved to her.

She ignored me.

One of the lads called out, "What are you looking at, you posh cow?"

Kelly was laughing. She lit a cigarette and blew smoke in the boy's face.

"Ignore them," said Tom under his breath.

I glanced back at Kelly. She was saying something into one of the boy's ears.

As we passed the slide, the boy shouted out, "Kelly says you're a fat bitch!"

28

David Goldsmith puts the notebook face down on the end of the bed, its peacock blue cover splayed like a butterfly's wings. He lifts Anna's hand from the bed, checking her pulse – still too fast. He reads the numbers on the oximeter and looks at the cardiac monitor.

He looks at Anna's face – peaceful, like a baby. The arched bow of her top lip, her thick, curled eyelashes, her wonderful dark eyebrows. Her hair is spread across the pillow like black silk. He touches her face, his hand tracing the line of her cheek, smooth and flawless. Snow White in her glass coffin: rosebud mouth and raven hair. Anna Frances Goldsmith. Anna-Panna. Anna-Pianna. Princess Pan-Anna.

He opens her eyelids. Her pupils are dark and huge. She does not see him. She is far, far away. He wonders where she has gone in her dreams? What is she thinking? Will she hate him when she wakes up? Does she have any idea how much he loves her? Perhaps if he kisses her she will wake up.

His wife is dozing in the chair. She looks worn out. David tucks a hospital blanket round her knees. Good bedside manner. Such a nice doctor.

He sits by Anna. This is all new. Today he is the patient, not the doctor. Or rather, the patient's father. The impatient father. The waiting is intolerable. Waiting in limbo. Not knowing.

He picks up the book again and leafs through it. This is his daughter. His secret daughter. The one he barely knows.

29

Wednesday August 21st

Went to the Dales. Melanie came, and Angus. They hardly spoke to each other. It must be the most slow-moving romance on record! I wish Melanie would just go on and ask him out. She says she isn't sure if she fancies him any more. She said he looked a bit puny with his clothes off!

We went up Pen-y-ghent – the steep way. Melanie was a bit subdued.

"What did you do while we were in France?" I said.

"Not much," she said. She looked very brown.

"How come you're so tanned?" I asked.

We were sitting beside the waterfall at Stainforth, on the rocks. Tom and Angus were jumping off the tree roots. Angus splashed me so that my T-shirt got wet. It was a bit revealing. Angus kept looking at my boobs.

Melanie didn't answer. She changed the subject. "Tom's got nice legs," she said, as he climbed up the rocks out of the water. "The water looks like tea," she said.

"It's the peat," I said. Know-all, I thought. "Was

it really hot in Wales then?" I said.

"Yeah," said Melanie.

She was wearing a leather bangle that I hadn't seen before. It looked Spanish, or Portuguese. Hayley's got one similar. I saw it once when we were trying on clothes in her bedroom.

"That's nice," I said, fingering it.

I thought of Hayley and I felt my stomach clench as though someone had squeezed me inside.

"Have you seen Hayley?" I asked. *The question came out automatically. Autosuggestion.*

Melanie looked startled. She looked away and fiddled with the strap on her sun top.

"I bumped into her in town one day," she said. *Then she asked, "Is there any coke left?"*

Mum was sitting beside the picnic bag in a big straw hat. She had her bare feet in the shallow pools at the edge of the river.

"Coke? Yes, love, it's here," she said. *She handed the bottle to Melanie. "Would you like a cup?"*

Melanie nodded. I rummaged in the bag.

"Is there any food left?" I said. *I found a squashed bag of crisps and some apples.*

Mum was looking across the river serenely. On the opposite bank there were ferns and yellow flowers. I sat beside her on the grass. She stroked the back of my hair. Mum's quite nice in the holidays, especially by the end of the summer when she's had six weeks to mellow out.

"Did you have a nice time in Wales, Melanie?" she said.

"Yes," said Mel.

"Nice weather?" said Mum.

"Yes . . . great weather."

"Are you looking forward to going back to school, Melanie?" Mum slid her sunglasses down her nose.

"Kind of," said Melanie.

"GCSE year," said Mum. "It's the important one, isn't it?"

I wonder how many times I'll hear that this year. GCSEs. GCSEs. Coursework. Coursework. Violin. Coursework. Violin. Exam practice. Work hard. Do well. Work hard. Do well.

I'm dreading going back to school. I wish it could be always summer.

Thursday August 22nd

Tom failed his A Levels. He needed two Cs and a D to get into Keele to do Geography. He got two Es and a U in Maths. Nick got two As and a B. He's going to Durham to do Law.

David Goldsmith thinks of Tom, results in hand, standing in the kitchen looking ashen-faced. He remembers how mad he was with him. How disappointed.

"Lazy sod!"

He hears his own voice and sees his jabbing finger prodding at thin air.

"If you'd got off your backside and applied yourself a bit . . . but no! Not you! Not Tom Goldsmith! You thought you'd just sail through, didn't you . . ."

Tom hadn't answered.

Frances had cried. Bitter tears.

How futile it all seems now. How inflated and out of proportion.

30

I rang Anna again at ten twenty-five. Surely someone should be back by now?

I got the answering machine. I put the phone down and dialled again. *Please* answer, Anna. *Please* pick up the phone.

"This is 867452 – the home of Frances and David Goldsmith and Anna. I'm sorry we're unavailable to take your call right now, but if you leave your name and number after the tone we'll get back to you very soon. *Beeeep!*"

I slammed down the receiver.

Guilt is a terrible thing. It eats at you, chews your insides. I couldn't settle. I kept hearing my own words in my head, pounding round and round like fists on a drum.

31

Frances Goldsmith stirs in her chair and stretches her arms. Her mouth feels silted up, like a furred kettle.

David is sitting on the other side of Anna's bed.

"How is she?" says Frances.

"No change," says David.

David is still reading Anna's diary. He rests the blue cover on his knees.

"I wasn't sure we should read it," says Frances. "She was holding it . . . in the bathroom . . . when I found her . . ." That picture again. It will haunt her. Anna on the cushions, white-faced and motionless.

"It doesn't sound like Anna," says David. He sighs and closes the notebook. "It's like reading something a stranger's written. I hardly recognise her . . . us . . ."

Frances rubs her eyes. "I recognise myself all too well," she says. She looks at David, "How far have you got?"

"Last summer," he says. "Tom's A Levels."

"Oh God." Frances breathes out heavily and slides her feet into her shoes. "I thought I'd start at the beginning," says Frances. "Start with the innocuous, harmless stuff first . . . save the grim truth till last. She'd been writing in the bathroom . . . before I found her . . . there was ink on the towels. I skipped all the slushy stuff about Nick, but I read the rest – every page. *Most* of it is awful! So much cruelty! So much misery!"

Frances squeezes her eyelids shut to hold back tears. She has cried too much already. Her eyes ache. She reaches into her bag. "There was this too," she says. "I couldn't bring myself to read it..." She hands the letter to David. "There are two more, one for that wretched Hayley Parkin and one for Melanie..."

David fingers it.

"You read it," says Frances. He unfolds the note.

Dear Mum and Dad,
I am sorry for the distress this is going to cause you. You will think I am selfish, that I haven't thought of you. You will think I have let you down – again.

But I cannot go on. My life is unbearable. I feel as if I am in a deep dark hole and the walls are pressing in on me. I am so lonely. Everyone hates me. I hate myself more and more. Each day gets worse.

I'm sorry for being a disappointment to you. I'm sorry I'm a useless daughter.

I have tried to do this with as little mess and fuss as possible. I hope you will forgive me.

Love, Anna

David reads it without speaking. Then he walks across to the chair and hands the note to his wife. Frances reads it too. She cannot hold back tears. They stream down her face and splash the page. Her hand gropes blindly for David and finding him, she laces her fingers tightly with his. When she has finished reading they sit together in silence.

32

Things were worse than ever in September, at the beginning of the new term, at the start of Year Eleven. Anna kept out of everyone's way. She started going to the library at lunchtimes. Hayley pursued her, like a dog with a rabbit.

It was dinnertime, at the end of the first week back. Anna came into the form room to get her bag.

"Aren't you coming, Anna?" said Hayley. "We're going to the ice-cream van." Hayley had her gang around her – Ruth Smith and Siobhan Reid and Joshua and all the other nobodys who hover in her slipstream. I was there too.

"Melanie's coming," said Hayley. "Aren't you?" She linked her arm through mine. There's an ice-cream van outside the school gates most lunchtimes.

"I haven't got any money," I said, looking at Anna.

"That's OK," said Hayley. "I'll buy you something." Then she said, "Nice bracelet, Mel. Is that the one you bought in Portugal?"

Anna looked at me sharply and then turned and left the room.

Hayley followed her down the corridor. "You're not going to the library, *again*, Anna?" she said in a really loud voice. "Aren't you clever enough?"

Anna ignored her.

"You're not very sociable this term Anna, are you?" Hayley was right behind her. Anna didn't turn round. "What's up, Anna? Don't you like us any more?"

Anna had reached the library door. Hayley was so close she had her face in Anna's hair.

"Cow!" Hayley said in a low voice.

I was alongside her. I could see Anna's knuckles gripping her bag. I saw Hayley stick her foot out and hook it round Anna's ankle so that Anna fell forward and bashed her face on the door.

"Ooops, sorry, Anna! Are you all right?" Hayley was smiling.

Anna didn't turn round. She pushed open the door and disappeared into the library.

Hayley linked arms with me again. "Her trouble is she's got no sense of humour," said Hayley. I said nothing to defend Anna. Hayley was marching me along the corridor towards the stairs. "Do you want a Magnum?" she said.

33

Anna asked me about Portugal. It was after orchestra. She was putting her violin into its case.

"Are you catching the bus home?" I asked. I could tell she was mad at me. She hadn't spoken to me all day.

"I suppose so," she said. She didn't smile.

We got off the bus and crossed the road towards the park. Anna was scowling. I remembered something Hayley had said: "Look at Anna! When she's cross her eyebrows join together in one thick black line. Her eyebrows are so bushy you'd think she'd pluck them!" I looked at Anna's eyebrows and smiled. I couldn't help it.

"What are you smiling at?" Anna asked.

"Aren't I allowed to smile?" I said.

"You went to the Algarve, didn't you? To the Parkins' villa? That's why you were so brown, isn't it? Your mum said it rained most of the time you were in Wales!"

Anna's eyes burned into me. I looked away.

"I don't see what it's got to do with you, Sherlock Holmes!" I said.

"Only that Hayley Parkin's declared World War Three against me and you're supposed to be my friend!" Anna looked as if she was going to cry.

"I *am* your friend," I said. It had a hollow ring to it. "Look, I didn't really want to go . . . Hayley persuaded me . . ."

It was a lie. Of course I'd wanted to go. A week in the sun with a private swimming pool all for free. Who was I kidding?

"I didn't even enjoy it!" I said. More lies. Actually, it was brilliant. Anna looked hurt so I lied again. "Hayley was in a huff for most of the week . . ."

The truth is, Hayley was actually nice – surprisingly nice, with no one there to pick on, and no audience to play to. That's the funny thing about Hayley. She can be so charming when she chooses to be. I even found myself wondering if it was Anna's fault – all the stuff at school.

"She brings it on herself," Hayley had said as we were lying by the pool.

"Who, Anna?" I had said.

"Who else?" said Hayley. "She's such a wind-up!"

I hadn't agreed, but I hadn't disagreed either.

Anna's violin case bashed against her leg. "I just don't see how you can be friends with her, Melanie," she said.

"So what are you saying, Anna?" I said, suddenly annoyed with her. "That I'm only allowed to be friends with you? Is that it? You have a monopoly do you?"

Anna flicked her hair off her face. "She's only using you, Melanie," she said. "She doesn't know the meaning of the word friendship."

"That didn't seem to bother you when she was hanging round with *you*!" I said.

We were going through the park, on the path between the chestnut trees. The ground was littered with spiky conker shells. I kicked one angrily.

"And besides –" I said. There was no stopping me now. She'd asked for it. "– you weren't exactly a brilliant friend all the time you were going out with Nick! You were quite happy not to see me then! Talk about using people!"

"That was months ago," Anna said.

"Is that supposed to make a difference?" I asked.

The handle of my clarinet case was cutting into my fingers. I changed it into the other hand. A squirrel ran across the path. We walked the rest of the way in silence and parted without saying goodbye.

I felt terrible. I was ashamed about Portugal. It felt sneaky, like cheating. And I regretted what I'd said about Nick. I'd have been just the same if Angus had asked me out. If.

I tried to be really nice to Anna to make up for being disloyal. I wanted to prove to her that I *was* her friend. Her best friend. That she could trust me.

She came to my house for a sleepover the next weekend. She slept in a sleeping bag on my floor. We talked till two in the morning about lads and clothes and things. Neither of us mentioned Hayley. I asked Anna if she still liked Nick. She said she was glad he'd gone away to university as she didn't have to see him any more. I guess that meant yes. Her brother Tom was thinking of moving out into a flat, she said, with a bloke called Damien. I asked if Tom was gay. "Oh yeah!" said Anna, laughing. I guess that meant no!

Mum made lots of food: cakes and scones and sandwiches with no tops on. "Just a bit of supper," she said, before we went to bed.

We were in the lounge, watching the telly. Mum put a tablecloth on the coffee table.

I wish she wouldn't fuss so much. Anna's parents just leave us to it when we go round there. I didn't tell Mum that. She has this thing about the Goldsmiths. How they think they're better than everyone else.

"Didn't she give you anything to eat?" Mum says, when I've been round at Anna's. ("She" is Mrs Goldsmith.)

"No, we just helped ourselves . . ." Mum had that face on. The one where she thinks something isn't good enough but she isn't going to say so.

Anna didn't eat much supper. She seemed to eat less and less. At school she never got a pudding any more and when it was chips she left half of them. She was getting thinner. Less voluptuous. Mum was watching her out of the corner of her eye, nibbling at a piece of flapjack. Mum hates people who are faddy about food.

34

Hayley was off school for nearly three weeks in the autumn term. She had glandular fever. The atmosphere was different without her. Less spiky. Less hostile. I noticed people talking to Anna more when Hayley was away, sitting near her in the cafeteria, including her in their conversations.

When Hayley came back she had to fight to re-establish herself, like a wild animal marking out its territory.

The usual jokes and taunts were wearing a little thin so Hayley started playing dirty. She told lies about Anna: "Ruth, Anna Goldsmith says your sister is a slag." ... "When you got told off in Maths, Joshua, you should have seen Anna Goldsmith laughing behind your back!" ... "According to Anna you'll never even manage a C grade in French, Claire." ... "Didn't you know about Anna Goldsmith and Mr Atkinson? I saw them in the stock cupboard at lunchtime! Didn't you know? It's been going on for months! I'm surprised the Head doesn't do something about it. You won't tell anyone will you?" ...

People are so gullible. They believed her.

35

It was November, just after half term. We were getting changed for PE. Anna had new trainers.

"Nice trainers, Anna," said Hayley. "Can I have a look?"

Hayley was on the other side of the changing room. There was a horrible smell of stale clothes and sweat. "Here?" said Hayley. She put her hands out to catch and nodded to the shoe Anna was holding.

Anna threw the shoe to Hayley. Hayley looked at the trainer, turning it round in her hands. "Nice," she said. "How much were they?"

I looked at Anna. I could tell she didn't want to say.

"Forty-nine ninety-nine," she said. She said it with a northern accent, dropping the "t"s in forty and ninety. Anna's done that a lot recently. You'd hardly know she was from "down south" now.

"Is that all?" said Hayley.

Anna pulled her cycling shorts on.

Hayley sniffed the inside of Anna's shoe, inhaling in deep gulps and pulling a face as she did it. "At least they don't smell, Anna," she said with a grin. "Yet!" Then she said, "They sell odour eaters at that shop near your house, don't they, Mel? The shop that does shoe repairs and key cutting. I noticed them, the other day. Do you know anyone who needs a pair, Melanie?"

Several people were laughing. Anna was tying her hair back in a scrunchy.

"Ho ho, Hayley," I said, glaring at her.

"Can I have my shoe back?" said Anna quietly.

"Sorry, Anna, I didn't quite hear. What did you say?" Hayley turned her head on one side and strained towards Anna as though she was hard of hearing.

"I said, can I have my shoe back?" said Anna, a little louder.

"What?" said Hayley. "I didn't catch that!"

Anna said it again in a loud voice. Her face went red as she spoke.

"There's no need to shout, Anna! I'm not deaf!" said Hayley, smirking. Then she said "Here!" and she hurled the shoe straight at Anna.

It hit her in the face, right on the top of her nose. Anna yelped in pain.

"Oops! Sorry!" said Hayley.

Anna cupped her hands over her face. When she took her hands away her eyes were watering.

Hayley flounced past, taking the gold studs out of her ears. "Don't cry, Anna," she said in a snide voice. "Melanie will kiss it better." She gave me a patronising look and swung open the changing-room door.

* * *

It was pouring with rain, so instead of hockey we did circuit training in the gym. We had to work in pairs, timing each other and counting sit-ups and step-ups. I worked with Anna. She was much better than me.

"Nice sit-ups, Anna," said the teacher. "Nice muscle control, Hayley. Come on Melanie, a bit more effort, please."

We had our feet tucked under the wall bars. Hayley was doing step-ups on a bench to the side of us.

"You've lost weight," said Hayley to Anna. She said it in a stage whisper.

I saw a flicker of pleasure go across Anna's face. A trickle of sweat ran down her chest.

"Mind you don't get anorexic, won't you," Hayley said, sounding concerned. "You don't want to end up all skin and bone!" She glanced sideways at Ruth Smith and they smiled conspiratorially.

"Anna-rexic!" said Ruth, with a snort of laughter.

At the end of the lesson we had to put the apparatus away. Anna and I were lifting the balance beam. It's very heavy and its base is like an iron bar running at right angles to the beam. You have to keep your feet well clear of it.

"Straight backs, bent knees, girls," said the teacher.

"We don't want any injuries."

"I think the circuit training's already given me plenty of those!" I said.

"Plenty of what?" said Hayley, coming into earshot. She was dragging a crash mat across the floor.

"Injuries," I said.

"Let me take that, then," Hayley said. She took hold of my end of the beam.

"It's OK, Hayley. I can manage," I said firmly.

Hayley dug her elbows into me, pushing me out of the way. "You take the mat, Melanie," she said.

Anna was walking backwards towards the wall. She had her legs splayed to keep her feet free from the beam's iron base. Hayley grabbed the beam and began to walk too fast.

"Slow down!" said Anna.

"Sorry!" said Hayley sarcastically. She slowed down. I turned and dragged the crash mat in the other direction.

"Well done, girls, put the beam in the corner, up against the wall," I heard the teacher say.

I leaned my crash mat up against the others and turned round. Hayley was backing Anna into the corner, pinning her against the wall of the gym. I walked towards the gym door. Most people were already in the changing-rooms. The teacher turned her back, stacking stopwatches in a box. Hayley suddenly jabbed the beam so that she rammed Anna up against the wall.

"Careful," Anna said quietly.

Hayley pushed again so that Anna's ribcage was trapped between the beam and the wall. Anna flinched, wriggling herself free.

"It needs to go to the right a bit, Anna," said Hayley innocently. "We'll put it down on the count of three. OK?"

I guessed what was coming.

"One, two . . ." Hayley dropped her end of the beam with a jerk on the count of two so that the iron bar came down on Anna's foot.

Anna yelped.

"Sorry!" said Hayley. "My hand slipped! Are you all right?"

Anna crumped to the floor and held her foot. The teacher came across.

"I trapped her foot by accident, Miss," said Hayley. She smiled knowingly at me.

What could I say? "She did it on purpose, Miss?" It didn't sound very likely. Hayley would deny it.

Anna's eyes filled with tears. She unlaced her shoe. There was a red mark on the top of her foot. The teacher rubbed it.

"Can you move your toes?" she said.

Anna wriggled them.

"I think you'll live," said the teacher. "You'll be

more careful next time, won't you?"

Anna wiped her eyes with the back of her hand.

36

It was late November when I first realised Anna was slashing herself. There are some girls in our year that make themselves bleed just for "fun" – to get attention. They scratch their arms with compass points and bits of glass and then show everyone the scabs. It's gross. I'm surprised they don't get hepatitis. (My mum brought home a leaflet about that as well.)

With Anna it was different. She wasn't doing it to impress anyone. She was doing it because she wanted to harm herself.

It was a Wednesday. Anna came to my house after school. We were in my bedroom. We were supposed to be doing Geography homework, drawing a pie chart about world population growth.

Anna was in a bad mood. She'd had a row with her mum before school and Hayley had been getting at her all day – not that that was anything new.

Mum was out. She works late on a Wednesday. I took a tin of biscuits upstairs. Anna wouldn't have one. She was eating less and less all the time. She'd started bringing an apple to school for her lunch instead of having a school dinner – just an apple. Imagine.

"Anna," I said, stuffing my face. "You should eat. You'll waste away."

"Stop hassling me, Melanie!" she said.

"Sorr-*ree*!" I said. I laughed but Anna didn't laugh back.

"I wish everyone would get off my case!" she said. "Everyone goes on at me all the time!"

She started doodling on her Geography file. I ate another custard cream. Anna read out what she'd written: "Hayley Parkin is a cow!" As she said cow she stabbed her finger with her pencil point.

"Careful," I said. "You'll get lead poisoning!"

"It didn't break the skin," Anna said. She dropped the pencil and started unbuttoning the cuff of her school blouse. "Not like this," she said suddenly.

She pushed her blouse up above her elbow. There was a long red scab running down her arm – three inches at least – all puckered and crusty.

"God, Anna!" I said. "How did you do that?" I thought maybe she'd had an accident or been scratched by the cat or something.

"Do you really want to know?" she said. She tossed her hair out of her eyes.

I didn't answer.

Anna took a tiny tin out of her pencil case. Without

speaking she prised off the lid and took out a razor blade.

"Shit, Anna! What have you got that for?" I asked.

"I'll show you," she said.

I laughed. "Anna," I said. "Don't be stupid . . ."

She was sitting on my bed. Without looking at me, she pushed up her other sleeve and positioned the razor blade against her skin, just below her elbow.

"Anna, stop it! That's gross!" I said. "Anna, for God's sake . . ."

She pressed the razor blade down and scored into her flesh. A thick, bright trickle coursed down her arm. Anna watched it.

"It doesn't hurt," she said, half-smiling. "You'd be surprised how little it hurts."

The blood was streaming down her arm, heading for my bed. I grabbed a box of tissues off my dressing table and thrust a wad of them at her.

"It makes a bloody mess, though! God, Anna!" I said. I thought about my mum, what I'd say if she found blood all over the duvet.

Anna was holding the tissues on to her arm. A large red patch was seeping across the whiteness, like something growing – like a disease spreading.

Anna said nothing. I had a stronge urge to slap her – to tell her to stop feeling sorry for herself and being such a little drama queen. But I was scared too. There was a weird look in her eyes – like she was falling off the edge, going a bit crazy. At the same time I wanted to hug her and mop up the blood and make it all better.

Anna lifted the sodden tissues off her arm. My stomach lurched. The cut was deep and open and blood was still oozing from the length of it.

"It looks as if you need stitches," I said.

"It'll be all right," Anna said.

I took some more tissues from the box. "Hadn't you better run it under the tap?" I suggested.

"It will hurt then," Anna said.

"You should have flipping thought of that!" I said.

We went into the bathroom and Anna held her arm under the cold tap. A scarlet river ran down the side of the bath. Anna grimaced and bit her lip. I rummaged in the bathroom cabinet and found cotton wool and plasters.

"Here, I'll patch you up," I said.

"Thanks," said Anna, without looking at me. She sat down on the side of the bath. Tiny drips of blood fell to the floor and splattered the tiles. "Sorry about the mess," she said quietly. Then suddenly she was crying. Fat messy tears were running down her face. "Oh God," she sobbed. "I can't stand it. I can't stand it!"

I didn't need to ask what she meant. I wiped her face on a towel.

"It's like scratches," Anna said. She pressed her

nails into the back of her hand. "Like she's digging her nails into me. Just little scratches but the same spot every time so that it hurts more and more each time . . . bleeds more and more . . . and the marks get deeper and deeper. It's like a wound. Like a wound deep inside that no one can see. Mel, it hurts so much . . ."

I held her, just like I had on New Year's Eve. One hand holding a pad of cotton wool on to her arm, the other hand stroking her hair.

"It's all right, Anna," I said. "Sssh, it's all right."

I wish it had been all right. I wish that had been the end of it.

By the time Mum came home Anna was gone. I tidied up as best I could but Mum misses nothing.

"What's the blood on the bathtowel?" she asked.

"I had a nosebleed," I said.

"In the bathroom?" Mum was looking at me suspiciously, boring into me with her eyes.

"I had a bath," I said. "When I got in from school."

37

Monday November 18th

Hayley tripped me up when I was giving out the science books. No one saw. It was the start of the lesson. People were still moving about and Mrs Forbes was talking to the lab technician. Hayley was on the back benches. Siobhan was with her, and Ruth Smith. As I went by, Hayley stuck her foot out. I hit my head on a stool and dropped the whole pile of books. They scattered all over the floor.

Mrs Forbes looked up. "Careful, Anna!" she said. "Come on, get those books picked up."

I bent down to gather the books.

"Miss, shall I help her?" I heard Siobhan's voice.

"Thanks, Siobhan. Right, Year Eleven, if I could have hush now please . . ."

Siobhan crouched down near me and started putting science books on the pile. She smiled a really sickly smile at me. "You're getting very clumsy, Anna," she whispered. "Are you feeling OK?"

I didn't answer.

One of the books was right over by the wall. As

I reached out for it, Siobhan trod on my fingers. I heard Hayley laugh.

"Ow!" I yelped.

"Sorry, Anna," said Siobhan. She said it just loud enough for people to hear.

"Come on girls, hurry up!" said Mrs Forbes.

I looked up and saw Ruth Smith smirk.

No one was in when I got home. I got a razor blade from Dad's drawer and shut myself in the bathroom. I sat on the bathroom chair and pressed the blade into my arm, into the fleshy part above my elbow. It made a dent, but it didn't break the skin. My skin looked pale and squashy, like sausages that haven't been cooked. I took the razor away. There was a thin grey line on my arm where I'd been pressing the edge of the blade, like a thread.

Then I did it. One quick gash, downwards, like striking a match. It was easy. It hardly hurt at all. There was a lot of blood. I wrapped a flannel round it.

Afterwards, as the blood started to congeal, it throbbed. I didn't mind the pain. It was bearable because I had caused it. I had done the damage. I wasn't just the victim. It made me feel powerful. For once it was Me that was controlling something.

I could see the blood. I could see the torn skin. It was real. More real than the damage that Hayley does inside me. That's all in my mind. It doesn't really exist. Sticks and stones can break my bones, but words will never hurt me.

In the Middle Ages, they cut people to make them bleed if they were ill. I read that in a History book at school. Bloodletting, they called it. They thought that if they let some blood out they would let the disease out too. They believed they could bleed all the sickness out. Just let it all run out and flow away.

38

Tuesday November 19th

I got the results of my Grade Seven violin exam today. I was two marks short of distinction.

Mum said, "What a shame you only got a merit. Only two marks away." That was all she said. No congratulations or anything. At least she didn't say: "If you'd done more practice you'd have got a distinction," though I bet that's what she was thinking. Nothing I do is good enough. She always wants more of me.

Tom has moved out – lucky sod! He's gone to live in a flat with his friend Damien. He's got a job as a motor cycle courier, delivering parcels, and he isn't going to retake his A Levels. Mum and Dad think he's wasted his life. "You'll regret it!" Dad said. "Just you watch. You'll regret it!"

I wonder if Mum and Dad ever regret anything. They're so smug. So sorted.

Wednesday November 20th

Mum asked if I wanted to move into Tom's room.

"He's not dead!" I said. He might as well be, as far as Mum is concerned.

"I take it that's a no," Mum said. She was chopping up a salad. I didn't answer.

Mr Atkinson says I should get an A* grade in French to go with the ones I'm supposed to get in English, Maths and Music. Pile on the pressure, why don't you!

Mum keeps asking about coursework deadlines. "You are keeping up?" she said at breakfast time. "We're all expecting you to get super results, Anna." She paused and then she added, "We don't want you to mess up your life like Tom has."

"Not that she's likely to," said Dad beaming at me. "We're proud of you sweetheart," he said.

They haven't a clue! They haven't a flaming clue. To them I'm sweet, happy, successful, little Anna. Anna-Panna.

Why haven't they noticed? Why can't they see what's going on? Why can't they stop it?

I cut myself again today – on the other arm, lower down. It bled more than before. I think I cut deeper. The other cut is healing fast. There's a long sugary scab that I want to pick. I can feel it at school if I run my finger down the sleeve of my blouse. It's like a ridge. Hayley was laughing at me today. Something about my bottom when I walk. I didn't listen. I touched my arm and thought of the blood oozing down, salty and warm.

Tuesday November 26th

Hayley kicked me this morning. Just kicked me. I was walking past her in the form room and she jabbed her foot against my shin. She made no attempt to disguise it. No pretence of an accident.

Why does no one notice? Why does no one say anything?

I have four cuts on my arms now, two on each side. The first one has lost its scab and healed into a neat purple line. The skin is shiny, like the skin on a black grape – plump and fragile looking.

I was in the bath tonight and Mum wanted to get to the laundry bin. Normally she just knocks and comes in. We never lock doors. We're all very uninhibited. Mum thinks that's more healthy. I'd locked the door so she wouldn't see my arms.

"Anna?" she said. "Can I get in to get the washing?"

"Hang on," I said. "I'm in the bath."

"I'll only be a moment," said Mum.

"I'm just washing my hair," I said. "Hold on!"

I wrapped myself in a big bath sheet before I opened the door and hugged it tight round my shoulders. Mum looked surprised.

"Are you all right?" she said.

"Fine," I said. I'm getting pretty good at lying.

Wednesday December 4th

Mum was asking about Christmas. She asked if I wanted a new party dress or did the one she bought last year still fit. I haven't worn it since New Year's Eve.

"I think it's too tight," I said.

"Really?" said Mum. "I wouldn't have thought you'd grown that much and you've been losing weight recently. Too much weight, if you ask me . . ."

"I'm fat, Mum!" I said. "My bum is huge!"

"Nonsense!" said Mum cheerily. "Go and try it on! We'll have a look . . ."

I thought of the strappy shoulders. All that bare flesh. My arms. Mum would see my arms. I tried to change the subject.

"I don't think I'll wear party dresses this year anyway, Mum," I said. "They're not really my style any more." Mum looked disappointed.

"Why not?" she said. "You looked so gorgeous in it last year."

"Nick didn't think so!" I said stroppily. I don't know why I said that. It's not as if I've been pining for Nick or anything. Actually, I haven't thought about him for ages.

Mum pulled a knowing face and said, "Ahh," with a nod of her head. She almost looked relieved. As if she'd cracked it, solved the puzzle, confirmed her suspicions. That was why her daughter looked so miserable and exhausted. It was boyfriend troubles. She was still getting over that nice Nick Simpson. Such a pity. Such a nice boy.

Mum left the room with her sympathetic face on, relieved that she'd sussed it.

If being dumped by Nick was all I had to worry about, life would be simple.

Maybe I should tell someone about Hayley. Maybe it's time to blow the whistle. But who would I tell? Who would believe me? And tell them what? That she calls me names? That she laughs at me? That sometimes she trips me up accidentally on purpose? Big deal!

39

Frances Goldsmith is reading Anna's diary again. Her misgivings about trespassing, about intruding into Anna's secret world are long gone. Now she reads hungrily, with a mounting sense of outrage.

David has gone in search of coffee and something to eat. It is 5.00am. Anna is much the same. Still in a coma. Still peaceful and pale. Still under close scrutiny.

Frances looks at the marks on her daughter's arms. Most of them are fading now. Thin silver trails where the flesh has knit itself better and, on the more recent wounds, dull purple stripes, like lash marks. Thank God Anna had stopped doing that. Thank God it had all stopped. Except that, apparently, it hadn't.

David arrives with plastic cups full of machine coffee and some triangles of buttered toast on a canteen plate. "I got these, too," he says, pulling something wrapped in cellophane from his pocket. "Chocolate chip cookies . . . No change?"

"No change," says Frances. Laying Anna's notebook across her knees, she sips the coffee. Closing her eyes, she remembers.

* * *

It was the Christmas holidays, the ones just gone. David went off skiing for a few days with some colleagues from work.

Frances was exhausted from a hectic term at school. All she wanted to do was sleep, but David's parents were coming for Christmas and the house was a mess.

Anna was surly. She stayed in her room most of the time and didn't want to do anything.

Frances had suggested she make some Christmas decorations like she usually did. Anna said she didn't feel like it.

"Why don't you make some of those lovely Christmas biscuits – the ones with chocolate on top? They were delicious last year," Frances suggested.

"No one will eat them," Anna said.

Frances had made a *big* effort. She'd taken Anna shopping. Anna had hardly spoken to her. She'd asked her to help get Tom's room ready for Grandma and Grandad. Anna had flounced about and sulked so much that Frances had done it herself.

She'd tried so hard to be patient. To be tactful. Not to rub Anna up the wrong way. Then Tom had called by with a bin liner full of dirty washing and she'd blown her top with both of them.

The next day Anna didn't get up till lunchtime. That was unusual for Anna. She'd always been an early riser, like David. Bright and cheery at seven in the morning – not like Tom, who'd had to be dragged from his bed every morning in time for school.

Frances had knocked. Anna hadn't answered. Frances had gone in and pulled the curtains. It was nearly one. Anna was still sleeping. She was face down, hugging her pillow, the way she'd slept ever since she was a baby. She was wearing a cotton nightdress with short sleeves. The sleeves had ridden up in the night so that all of her arms were exposed.

Frances hadn't seen straight away. She had bent to pick a towel off the floor. "Anna," she had said gently. The light was poor. It was one of those winter days when the sun never quite rises. Frances had switched on Anna's bedside light. And then she'd seen. Great red gash marks. Scabs as long as pencils. Purple tracks, like zips.

Anna had opened her eyes and seen her mother's face. Quickly she'd thrust her arms under the duvet.

"Mum!" she said. "I've asked you not to come in without knocking!"

Frances hadn't moved. She felt as if she might be sick.

"I did knock," she said quietly. Then she'd said calmly, "What have you done to your arms, Anna?"

"Nothing." Anna rolled over in bed and turned her back to Frances.

"Anna, don't be stupid," Frances said. "Show me your arms."

Anna didn't answer.

"Anna? Anna, please will you tell me what's going on?"

Still no answer.

"Anna! Don't—"

"Just go Mum! Don't interfere! This is *my* room and it's private!"

Frances didn't move. She felt her calmness ebbing away.

"Just bloody go!" Anna shouted.

"Don't be rude, Anna!" Frances said. She sounded bossy. Angry. Confrontational. This wasn't how she'd handle something like this at school. There, she would be diplomatic and cool. Why was it so much easier to deal with other people's children than it was to deal with your own?

She tried again, more quietly. "Anna, please will you talk to me . . ."

"What's the point? You never listen!" Anna had pulled her pillow over her head.

"That's not fair, Anna."

"Life's not fair! Nothing's fair!" Anna sat up and threw the pillow at the wall. It hit a picture in a frame and the frame fell to the floor and broke.

"Shit!" said Anna. Frances said nothing. Anna swung her legs off the side of the bed and stood up. Her hair fell on to her shoulders. She hooked it angrily behind her ears.

Frances looked away. She took a deep breath. "What's not fair, Anna?" she said softly.

"Life's not fair!" said Anna again. "My life's not fair! The whole thing is *crap*!" She'd never spoken like this to her mother before. It was like a dam bursting.

Anna picked up a shoe and threw it at the wall. "Bloody hell!" she screamed. A mobile of tropical fish brushed against her head and snagged in her hair. Anna reached up and ripped it from the ceiling. "Nobody likes me!" she yelled. "Everybody picks on me! Everything I do is wrong!"

"Anna, that's not true! Lots of people—"

"What do you know about it?" shrieked Anna, throwing the tangled fish on to her bed. "You're not there every day, watching. Watching the smirking and the dirty looks! Hearing all the sarcastic comments! Anna Goldsmith this! Anna Goldsmith that!" Anna stared at her mother, her eyes blazing with rage. "Go on then!" she shouted.

"Go on what?" said Frances helplessly.

"Go on! Tell me I'm overreacting! Tell me I'm being too dramatic! Tell me I'm imagining things! Tell me I'm paranoid! That's what Melanie says! 'Lighten up, Anna! Don't take it so seriously! Just ignore her!' "

Anna's cheeks were bright red. She looked as if she would burst with anger.

"Ignore who?" said Frances, looking straight at her.

"Hayley!" said Anna. She pulled her dressing gown

off the chair. *"Hayley bloody Parkin!"*

As she said Hayley's name, Anna made a sound like a wounded dog and sank to the floor. She pulled the dressing gown over her head and crooked her knees up to her chest. Then she sobbed. Loud animal sobs.

Frances sat on the floor, at a loss to know what to say. At last she inched across the carpet and pulled the dressing gown off Anna's head. Anna slumped towards her so that Frances was cradling her in her lap.

"Oh God," Frances said, stroking Anna's wet cheeks. "Oh my baby."

"Don't make me go back to school, Mummy," said Anna, as the sobs subsided. "Don't make me go back! Please don't make me go back . . ."

40

After Anna's mum found out about her arms – and Hayley Parkin – Anna sort of collapsed. She went to bed and just slept for days on end. Her mum said she was "totally exhausted".

I went round with her Christmas present. I'd bought her a silver bracelet and some bath foam. Anna was sitting up in bed with lots of teddies round her. She looked a bit spaced out.

"Happy Christmas!" I said. I gave her the present.

"Thanks, Mel," she said.

"Open it if you like," I said. I sat down on the edge of the duvet.

"OK," Anna said. She peeled the wrapping paper off very carefully, without tearing it. "It's nice," she said. "Thanks." Then she said, "Sorry I haven't got you anything . . . I haven't been to the shops or anything . . ."

"It's all right," I said. "Don't worry about it." There was a pause and then I said, "Nice bears!" I picked up one of the teddies and rubbed its ears.

Anna almost smiled. "I'm regressing," she said. "Back to childhood. Bears and stuff."

I didn't laugh. I wasn't sure if it was meant to be a joke or not.

"I got a Christmas card from Angus," I said. It was a safe thing to talk about.

"Did you send him one?" said Anna.

"Of course!" I said.

Anna grinned. She reached up to brush her hair out of her eyes and I saw her arms for the first time since the day she cut herself at my house. We'd never talked about it again. Anna saw me looking, so she pulled her sleeve right up to her shoulders. She looked as if she'd been sliced up. I tried not to look too shocked.

"Was your mum mad?" I asked. "My mum would have gone ballistic."

"No," said Anna. "She wasn't – surprisingly." She let her sleeve drop and then she said, "My dad was a bit freaked out. He said it was a wonder I hadn't infected myself. I told him I washed the razor blade each time!"

Anna slid the silver bracelet on to her wrist. "It's nice," she said, again. Then she said, "Did you buy Hayley Parkin a present?"

My skin went prickly. "No," I said, quickly.

"What did she buy you?" Anna asked.

I felt myself blush.

"Just a tape," I said. Actually Hayley bought me a CD and a huge bar of Dairy Milk. I wanted to give it back to her and tell her to stuff it, but I didn't. I just said thanks and smiled politely. Melanie

Blackwood. Spineless moron.

Anna changed the subject. "Mum and Dad are being really nice," she said. "Mum's going to go into school the first day back and sort everything out. She says the way to tackle bullying is to confront it head on. She says Hayley probably doesn't realise how upset she's been making me and that she needs to be enabled to see how her behaviour is affecting other people. Dad says bullies are often sad, insecure people and that understanding why they do the things they do is halfway to sorting it out. I'm so relieved I finally told them!"

Anna's face brightened as she spoke. She looked like a little kid.

I wanted to cry. I said nothing.

41

Mrs Goldsmith did go into school. I'm not sure exactly what happened. Apparently she spoke to the Deputy Head and she spoke to our Head of Year and then *he* fixed up some meetings with Hayley and Mr and Mrs Parkin.

The teachers were surprised. Anna Goldsmith was so outstanding, so confident, so articulate. Surely she could stand up for herself. Surely she was a match for anyone.

And Hayley Parkin wasn't an obvious bully. She was bright. She was attractive. Sometimes she had too much to say for herself and she was a bit cheeky to teachers. But she worked reasonably hard and she knew when to suck up to people. Hayley's parents said Anna Goldsmith must be exaggerating. Hayley wasn't nasty by nature. Everyone knew she was popular and well-liked.

What the teachers don't know, and what the Parkins choose not to see, is that Hayley Parkin is devious. She's sly. She manipulates people. People are shit scared of her.

Even in junior school she could control other kids. There, it was more blatant. She made rings round people in the yard – linked hands with other children and trapped victims inside the circle. Then she'd taunt them: "You can't get out! I bet you can't get out!"

I remember her doing that to me – trapping me inside the interlocking arms: "Mel-an-ie Black-wood! Mel-an-ie No-good! You can't get ou-ut! I bet you can't get ou-ut!"

Anna was moved out of our form. I was moved too, to keep her company. Hayley was put on special report and watched closely for a while. The teachers thought they'd dealt with it. Everything was civilised and pleasant again.

Sometimes personality clashes occur. It's just one of those things. No need to overreact. No need to blow it up out of all proportion. That was what they said. That was what they hoped.

42

Frances Goldsmith thought she'd done the right thing. Openness was always for the good – bring things out into the light of day.

And the situation *had* seemed to get better. Anna's work had improved, she'd appeared to be concentrating better again, her teachers said she'd looked happy enough in school . . .

A nurse checks Anna's temperature. "Still high," she says, writing on her chart.

Frances Goldsmith fidgets in the chair and unwraps a chocolate chip cookie. She has Anna's diary open on her knees. She starts to read again.

Wednesday January 8th
New year. New term. New life.

So far so good. I only saw Hayley once today and she ignored me. The teachers are keeping us apart, like dogs in a ring. Mrs Mullen put Hayley and me in different groups in English when we were using tape recorders. She sent my group out to work in the corridor, as far from Hayley as possible. Mr Robinson – my new form teacher – keeps asking me if I'm OK and teachers keep smiling at me for no reason.

Melanie says Hayley said Mrs Parkin said it was all a big fuss about nothing. It seems odd now to think I was so upset. Perhaps it was my hormones!

Thursday January 9th

Snow today – about three inches. Some of the teachers didn't make it into school so lessons were a bit disrupted. Great excuse to doss!

Ace violin lesson this afternoon. I played really well. Mum says I should try and do Grade Eight before Easter, before all the exam pressure starts.

I saw Nick tonight. He came to see Tom. I answered the door. "Tom's moved out," I said. "Didn't you know?" I gave him Tom's phone number. "How's university?" I asked.

"Great," he said. "How's school?"

"Fine," I said.

He looked a mess. I didn't fancy him any more. I can't think what I ever saw in him, actually.

"Still playing tennis?" he said.

"Not in this weather!" I said. "I'd better go."

I shut the door. He left. I rang Mel and told her he'd been.

"Perhaps he'll ask you out again," she said.

"As if!" I said.

Friday January 10th

So much for the new start. I suppose it was too good to last. There was a message in my RE book: Anna Goldsmith is a grasser. *"Show it to the teacher," Melanie said. I didn't. I put it in the bin. This time I'm going to ignore her.*

Monday January 13th

Another note – slipped into the pocket of my PE bag. One word in big purple letters: Blabber.

In English we were talking about nicknames. Mrs Mullen was "brainstorming", jotting down our suggestions on the board.

"Do any of you use nicknames for each other?" she said. Then she added, "Repeatable ones only, please!"

"Starkey!" said someone.

"That's James Stark, is it?" said Mrs Mullen. "Yes, very good. Lots of nicknames are just a play on someone's name, aren't they?"

"Like Gazza," someone said.

"Exactly," said Mrs Mullen. She folded her arms and leaned against the desk. Then she said, "What about names that draw attention to some sort of characteristic, some feature?"

"My brother gets called Ginner, because he's got ginger hair," said Richard Price.

"Yes, that's a good example."

"There was a boy in our junior school that got called Toothy because his teeth stuck out."

"Jenna Parr used to get called Spaghetti because she was so tall and skinny!" Melanie said.

"OK," said Mrs Mullen. "Let's have some more. Just shout them out . . ." She turned her back and started scribbling down words people said.

"Blabber!" said Ruth Smith suddenly.

Mrs Mullen wrote it down. Chalk dust fell from the board, like smoke.

"Grasser!" said Joshua.

Mrs Mullen wrote again. Her hips wiggled as she wrote. Everyone was looking at me. Some of them were smiling.

"Dobber!" said Siobhan.

"What does that mean?" asked the teacher, turning round.

"Someone who dobs you in," said Joshua.

"Lands you in it," said Ruth, without a flicker of a smile. "Gets you into trouble, Miss. You know, like if someone told tales on you, accused you of doing something bad . . . you'd say 'She's dobbed me in, the cow!' "

A few people laughed. Mrs Mullen laughed too, trying to look hip and laid back.

Hayley wasn't laughing. She was staring straight at the board.

The sick feeling came back. That edgy, nervy,

not-sure-what's-coming-next feeling in the pit of my stomach. Melanie looked at me and smiled sympathetically. At least someone understands.

Tuesday January 14th

Stayed off school today. I told Mum I had a stomach ache. She looked worried.

"It's probably my period," I said. "I'll be OK with a hot water bottle on it."

"Are things still all right at school?" she asked anxiously.

"Yeah! Fine," I said.

I didn't want to worry her. She hasn't been sleeping very well. She looks very tired. Anyway, she's done all she can. Telling the teachers only makes it worse.

I watched daytime TV and ate chocolate biscuits. Mel came round after school. Angus has invited her to a party on Saturday. She had a stupid grin on her face.

"Why don't you come?" she said. "Nick might be there!"

"So?" I said.

"So Nick might be there!" she said, grinning at me.

"Mel," I said. "I really don't like him any more!"

"As if?" said Mel, laughing. I threw a cushion at her.

"Will Hayley be there?" I asked.

Melanie stopped laughing. "Maybe," she said.

"I don't think I'll come then," I said.

Thursday January 16th

I went back to school. I had no choice. Mum threatened me with the doctor. She made me eat breakfast. She thinks I'm going to become anorexic. I told her I eat plenty. I just eat when she isn't there. She believed me.

Hayley was passing notes in Science. When the notes reached Joshua he read them out in a hushed whisper. The teacher was setting up an experiment. She kept going in and out of the lab cupboard. She was blissfully unaware of what was going on. So much for close pupil-surveillance.

"Anna Goldsmith is a ... what?" said Joshua, pretending he couldn't read it. "Crybaby?" he said, looking puzzled. "That's a bit tight, Hayley," he said, pouting. He wobbled his bottom lip as if he was going to cry. "How dare you say such howibble things about nice Anna!" he said, creasing up his face and pretending to cry.

I acted as though I couldn't hear.

Another note arrived. "Anna! You're not!" said Joshua with mock surprise. He held the note up for me to see. Mummy's girl! *it said in Hayley's* writing. "Hayley, what a nasty cruel thing to say!" he said in a baby voice.

Hayley smiled.

I smiled too. I laughed in fact. Perhaps Mel had been right all along. Perhaps if I could take the joke, if I saw the funny side, if I saw that it was just a bit of fun . . .

Hayley's face changed, as if she'd taken off a mask. "I don't know what you're laughing at, Anna Grassy-gob Goldsmith!" she said coldly. Then she added, "It's no joke telling lies about someone, you know, Anna."

I looked round at the other kids but everyone looked away, noses in books. Even Melanie didn't look at me.

At afternoon break, Hayley followed me into the toilets. I was washing my hands. The bell went. The toilets emptied quickly. Hayley came out of a cubicle and started washing her hands beside me. She caught my eye in the mirror and smiled a horrible smile, showing all her teeth.

When I wake up in the night thinking about her, that's the face I see.

I looked away and turned to press the knob on the hot air drier. Suddenly Hayley was behind me. She grabbed a handful of my hair and yanked it backwards. I froze. She pulled harder till my scalp was smarting. Then she dug her nails into my arm and said, "If you go running to Mummy again, Anna, I might get really nasty."

I tried to pull my head away but she jerked it back again, twisting my hair around her fingers.

"Don't forget, Anna. Nobody likes you. You're a fat slag. You're a stuck-up cow. You're a cold bitch. You might be the teacher's pet but that won't do you much fucking good!"

She let go of my hair and pushed the back of my head so that I bashed my forehead on the hand drier.

I heard the toilet door slam and her footsteps in the corridor. I didn't move. I looked at myself for ages in the mirror. I looked so ugly and stupid. When I cry, my face puffs up like a tomato and my nose looks like a pig.

After a while I pushed my fingers down my throat and made myself sick. I wanted to cut myself but I didn't have anything sharp. I wanted to cut myself till I bled to death. Then she'd be sorry. Then they'd all be sorry.

43

Monday January 20th

Melanie says she's going out with Angus – sort of.

"How d'you mean, sort of?" I asked.

"Well he didn't ask me or anything, but he walked me home from the party and he snogged me and stuff..."

"Was he drunk?" I asked.

"Oh cheers!" said Melanie.

"Sorry, I didn't mean it like that," I said. "Has he phoned you since?"

"No..." Mel looked mad with me. We were by the lockers. She was fiddling with her clarinet case.

Hayley came round the corner with Siobhan and Ruth Smith. She saw me and started talking in a loud voice.

"It was just a one night stand," she said. "I don't suppose I'll see him again. Anyway he's going back to college. I don't want to get serious. He isn't really my type. Too swotty. More Anna's type. Oh hi, Anna!"

I turned the key in my locker.

"Hi, Mel!" Hayley laughed. "You missed a great party on Saturday, Anna. Did Tom tell you about it?"

"Tom?" I said. I wasn't sure if she meant my Tom so I said, "My Tom? Was he there?"

They all laughed, Melanie as well.

"Ask Siobhan!" said Hayley.

They all laughed again.

"Tell me about it!" said Siobhan. Then she turned her back to me and said under her breath, "He's a lot more fun than his sister!"

"He's such *a naughty boy!" said Hayley. "Better not tell Mummy, Anna!" Then she said, "Shame you couldn't come. Mel enjoyed it, didn't you Mel?" Hayley nudged Melanie's arm and Melanie blushed. "Nick was asking how you were," said Hayley, coming close to me.*

"Nick?" *I said, trying to sound cool.*

"He goes back to university tomorrow," *Hayley said, taking off her coat.*

"I didn't realise you and Nick actually* talked!" *said Siobhan.*

Ruth Smith gave a snort of laughter then she said, "Was that before *he put his tongue down your throat, Hayley?"*

Hayley smirked. I looked at Melanie. She was smiling.

"Or was it after you disappeared together, Hayley?" *said Siobhan. "Where* did *you go to all that time, Hayley?" she said. "You didn't go* upstairs *by any chance, did you?"*

Hayley was laughing. "You can talk, Siobhan!" she said.

Siobhan took a packet of cigarettes out of her bag and slipped them into her pocket. Hayley shoved her bag into her locker and they went off down the corridor together.

As she was going round the corner Hayley said, just loud enough for me to hear, "He reckoned he did more with me *in one night than he did with Anna in six months . . ."*

Siobhan glanced back at me and grinned.

"I thought Nick thought Hayley Parkin was a tart," I said when they'd gone.

"Perhaps he likes tarts these days," said Melanie.

That was all she said. Then she took her clarinet and walked off.

44

I rang Anna again on Saturday morning. Tom answered the phone. I was surprised to hear him.

"It's Mel," I said. "Can I speak to Anna please?"

"Oh," said Tom. There was a pause, then he said, "Don't you know?"

"Know what?" I said.

"About Anna," Tom said.

"What about Anna?" I asked.

"She's in hospital," he replied.

"Why?" I said.

"She took an overdose."

I gasped. "Is she . . . is she all right?" I asked tentatively.

"She's in Intensive Care," Tom said. "She's in a coma. Dad said something about her heart."

"God!" I said.

Tom's voice sounded shaky. "Anna's the last person I'd have expected—" he said.

I interrupted. "Can we visit? I mean, do you think I could visit?"

"I'm just going there now. Dad asked me to call home and collect some things . . . You've only just caught me . . . Shall I wait for you?"

I was still in my nightie. I got dressed quickly and

dragged a comb through my hair. Mum was in the kitchen making bacon sandwiches. I grabbed a banana.

"Where are you going?" she said, looking at me as if I had a green face or something.

"I'll explain later," I said, lacing up my boots.

45

Frances Goldsmith has almost reached the end of Anna's diary. The writing seems to be getting smaller. More scribbly. More blotchy, as though something has been spilt on the page.

Sunday February 9th

Mum and Dad argued all weekend. Mum seems more irritable and brittle than ever – if that's possible. Everything Dad said was wrong. She snapped at him every time he opened his mouth.

Dad shut himself in his study and she sat in the kitchen drinking wine and crying. I think she's finally cracking up. We're becoming a dysfunctional family. Becoming?

I stayed in my bedroom, writing. I wrote a poem about Hayley Parkin. It's called "Shrinking".

Shrinking

When she comes
I get smaller.
Shrinking, sinking.
She is a black cloud
A tower
A boulder,

Hard as stone.
When I hit out,
My hands bleed and sting.
Now I am hiding.
Now she won't see me.
I am invisible
I am a vapour,
A phantom, a ghost.
Soon I won't exist at all.
Soon I will be gone.
Here is a hole.
Now I am falling
Falling and falling
Deeper and deeper
Darker and darker.
The circle of light,
Far above me
Smaller and smaller
And smaller.
Too late to shout for help.

46

Tuesday February 11th

Mr Holmes, the Head of Year, had a chat with me today. Me and Hayley Parkin. He called us into his office during morning break. We had to sit side by side on comfy chairs.

"So, girls," he said. "How are things between you two, now? Have you sorted out your differences?"

Hayley smiled at me with fake sincerity. "Things are fine, now, Sir," she said.

"Anna?" he said.

I looked at him. Wordless and dumb. What good were words? Sticks and stones may break my bones . . .

Hayley jumped straight in. "It was only ever a joke, Sir," she said. "Anna just overreacted, I think, didn't you, Anna? But we're friends again, now, aren't we Anna?"

I didn't answer.

"Anna says she was feeling a bit uptight about coursework and things. There's so much pressure in Year Eleven, Sir. We all get a bit anxious now and then," Hayley said.

She was making it all up, and he believed her. He smiled approvingly.

I opened my mouth to protest but no words came out.

"Anna's the last person that needs to worry," said Mr Holmes with a smarmy look. "We're expecting great things of Anna Goldsmith."

It felt as though I was in a trap. That whichever way I moved I was caught. I felt tears welling up in my eyes, stinging the backs of my eyelids.

"You've made such a contribution to the school, Anna. We're all very proud of you."

Tears splashed down my face. I couldn't stop them. I hate crying in front of people. I wanted to get up off the chair and run. Run as far away as I could. Run until I found a hole to hide in.

Hayley Parkin put her arm around my shoulder and handed me a tissue from her bag. I felt my whole body clench as she touched me. "Poor Anna," she said. "I think it's the relief that everything's sorted out."

I stood up, clutching my bag. "Excuse me," I said, without looking at them.

As I shut the door I could hear Hayley saying, "Anna's a bit oversensitive. She takes things so seriously. We've tried to make her laugh, to bring her out of herself a bit . . ."

After break it was RE. Hayley sat behind me with Ruth Smith. We had to work in groups, in fours, to discuss whether abortion was ethically acceptable or not. We had some pamphlets to read.

Melanie and I ended up in a foursome with Hayley and Ruth. Everyone seemed to have forgotten that we were supposed to be being kept apart. I still had red eyes.

"What's up?" said Ruth.

"Nothing," I said, staring at the floor.

"You look like you've been crying," Ruth said.

"She has," said Hayley. "Haven't you Anna?"

I didn't answer.

Hayley continued, "She tried crying in front of Mr Holmes to get his sympathy. She thought if she did a crybaby act he'd feel sorry for her. Didn't you Anna?"

Still I said nothing.

"But it didn't work, did it?" Hayley sounded triumphant. "She just made a fool of herself, didn't you Anna? If you keep bursting into tears everyone will think you're going mad, Anna. They'll think you need therapy, that you're going round the bend." She made a loony sign with her finger against her head. Ruth laughed. "They'll think you need to see a shrink . . . like your Mum!" Hayley said.

I looked up. Hayley was making a face at Melanie.

"Just leave off, Hayley," said Melanie. "Drop it!"

Hayley smiled. "Oh dear," she said. "Wasn't I meant to say that, Mel? Was it confidential?" Then she said, "It's just . . . Melanie says her mum said your mum had a prescription for antidepressants. Is that the stress of her job, Anna?"

Hayley looked at me as if she was concerned. I wanted to punch her in the face. I wanted to kick her teeth in. Extreme provocation, Sir. Self defence.

I didn't, of course. I ran out of the room in tears, like a crybaby. I went to Mr Holmes's office. I was a grasser, a blabber, I was dobbing her in. I'd tell him. Tell him the truth. Tell it like it was. Tell him what was really going on.

I knocked on the door. No one answered.

A Sixth Former went by. "He's teaching," she said. "In room eight."

I ran to the toilets and locked myself in a cubicle and cried until I was sick.

47

Friday February 14th

Valentine's Day. No valentines. Didn't get any. Didn't send any.

I thought Hayley was joking about the antidepressants but this morning I saw Mum with a jar of pills. "What are those?" I said.

She was sitting at the kitchen table with a cup of coffee. She's been off work this week. On the sick. I thought it was her migraine. She hid them in her dressing gown pocket. "Just something the doctor gave me," she said evasively.

"For migraine?" I asked.

"No, just to make me feel better... I haven't been sleeping well since..." She didn't finish her sentence – she didn't need to. Since she saw my arms. Since she knew her daughter was a basket case. Since she started hiding the kitchen knives.

"Don't tell Dad," she said in a childish voice. "Please Anna. Don't tell Dad. I don't want to worry him..."

I'm not likely to tell Dad. I never see him. His way of coping with "Anna's spot of bother at school" is to work more and come home less.

"Mummy will handle it," he said, at Christmas.

"Mummy will go into school and sort it all out. She's good at that sort of thing. Don't worry, Mummy will make it better." He'd kissed my nose, like he used to when I was small.

48

Saturday February 15th

Mel came over. She got a Valentine's card and she's convinced it's from Angus. She was going on and on about him. Angus this. Angus that. I couldn't be bothered to listen.

"Do you have to talk about Angus all *the time?" I said.*

"Soz!" she said sarcastically.

Mel is so preoccupied. I used to think she cared about me – about all that's been happening. The campaign. World War Three. Hayley Parkin's Reign of Terror! Now she seems bored by it.

I was lying on my bed. "Do you think Hayley Parkin would cry if I killed myself?" I asked.

"God, Anna!" she said. "What a morbid question!"

"I was joking," I said. Then I said, "If you were going to kill yourself, how would you do it?"

Mel looked worried. "You're sick, Anna," she said. She didn't smile.

"I'm only speaking hypothetically," I said. "Would you slash your wrists ... bleed to death?" I asked.

Mel didn't answer.

"Or would you take pills? Paracetamol? . . . No, that doesn't work. It just wrecks your liver. Dad told me that. Nothing happens at all, or else you die in agony of liver failure. It can take months – years even."

"Shut up, Anna," Mel said.

I ignored her. "What about hanging?" I asked. "Find a nice tree somewhere!" I picked my dressing gown cord off the floor and looped it round my neck.

Mel looked as if she was going to cry. She stood up.

"Don't worry, Mel," I said. "I was only joking." She sat down again, on my rainbow cushions. "With any luck, I won't have to kill myself at all. I'll just die of boredom listening to you drone on about Angus!"

Melanie didn't laugh. She got up and walked towards the bedroom door.

"It was a joke!" I said.

"What do you know about jokes, Anna?" said Mel. She had her hand on the doorknob.

"What's that supposed to mean?" I said, sitting up.

"Bye, Anna," said Mel. "I'm going."

"Where are you going?" I said. "Hayley Parkin's?"

"I don't go to Hayley Parkin's any more, actually Anna. And if I did, it would be none of your business."

I didn't answer.

Mel opened the door. "I really think you should let go of all this Hayley Parkin stuff, you know, Anna. You're only making it worse. You have to get past it. It's supposed to be all sorted out, anyway. Just ignore her. Don't take it all so seriously!"

Melanie left. I heard her feet on the stairs.

49

Tuesday February 25th

Hayley threw my pencil case at me. First she knocked it off my desk. Then she said, "Sorry, Anna, I'll pick it up. Here!" She threw it hard, right in my face. The zip scratched my eyebrow and made me bleed. More bloodletting. Soon there'll be nothing left inside me.

Friday February 28th

I wrote a piece in English about dying. Dying is like sleep. Dying is oblivion. We cease to be. We become a dream. The dream will be blue. Like the lake at the top of Helvellyn. Helvellyn was the last time I was happy. Dying will be happy. I will be on the top of the mountain, looking down at the blue lake under the blue sky. I will be serene. I will be peaceful. I will be the little thread of wispy cloud sitting over the fells, floating above the lake.

I am invisible

I am a vapour.

Mrs Mullen said it was a sensitive and imaginative piece and that I should read some Native American Indian myths. "You'd like them," she said. "You'd like the images . . . spirits

embodied in the landscape, in rocks and trees."
She said she'd bring me a book. She asked if she
could put my piece in the school magazine. I said
I'd rather she didn't. She looked disappointed. Silly
cow!

Wednesday March 5th

Hayley hit me in hockey. She made it look like an
accident. It isn't the first time she's done it. She
chopped my ankle with her stick.

I thought she'd broken the bone. I could hardly
walk. I had to leave the pitch.

I put paper towels on it, soaked in cold water.
Now it's swollen up like a grapefruit and there's
a huge black bruise.

I didn't tell Mum and Dad. I'm trying to
convince Mum that everything is fine, so she'll
stop worrying about me. She looked better today,
more cheery. More like her old coping self. She
cooked lasagne for tea. I didn't eat much. I felt
too sick.

Saturday March 8th

I wrote another poem today.

Underwater

I am underwater
Like an iceberg, nine tenths hid.
I am submerged,
Drowning,
In a blue world.
No one can see me.
Holding my breath
Not much air left.
Underwater.
Going down
Down, down,
Drowning.

50

Anna Goldsmith rolls her head and murmurs slightly. It is 9.14am, Saturday morning. Frances has been watching the numbers flash and change.

"Her consciousness level's lightening," says David.

"What does that mean?" says Frances.

"It means she's beginning to come out of the coma," says the nurse, reading Anna's screens. She pinches Anna's arm and Anna flinches and moans.

Frances feels a leap of joy. She looks at her husband. David's face is grave.

"We need to get that ET tube out immediately," he says.

"I'll phone the anaesthetist," says the nurse.

"I'll take it out," says David.

"She isn't your patient, Mr Goldsmith." The nurse is at her desk, telephone under her chin.

"No, but she is my daughter!" David is washing his hands at the sink and pulling on rubber gloves from a box at the end of the bed.

The nurse puts the phone down.

Frances speaks. "Shouldn't you wait?" she says very quietly. "You are very tired."

"Frances, if she wakes up with this tube down her throat she'll choke!"

Just then Roger Coldwell arrives. He nods to Frances. "Frances," he says with a brief smile. "David, let me do this, you've got enough to worry about," he says.

David sits down.

They pull the tube from Anna's airways and she gags slightly and groans.

"All right, darling," says Frances. "All right, Anna."

51

Anna is breathing more deeply now. Frances watches her chest rise and fall. She is less pale, less deathly. Her hands and feet twitch as if she is dreaming and sometimes she moves her lips. Frances sits close to her, stroking her daughter's hand. In her head she is repeating the same words over and over again, like a mantra: "Wake up, Anna. Anna, wake up . . ."

David has gone out for some air. Frances feels faint from tiredness and lack of food but she cannot bear to leave in case Anna should wake up. In case Anna should need her. She stares at the heart monitor, watching the identical mountain peaks draw themselves with monotonous regularity . . . *up* down up *down* . . . *up* down up *down* . . . *up* down up *down* . . . *up* down up *down* . . . She feels as if she is being hypnotised by the patterns. She blinks her eyes hard . . .

52

I meet Tom outside the Goldsmiths' house. He looks as if he hasn't been to bed.

"Thanks for coming," he says.

"It's OK," I say.

I toss my banana skin into a rubbish bin beside the park.

"Shall we catch a bus?" he says. "It'll be quicker." Then he says, "My car is off the road. I had an argument with a lamppost!"

We smile, but it feels a bit strained.

When we get on the bus Tom starts talking. "I just can't understand it," he says. "Anna! . . . Why?"

I don't say anything. Where do you start?

"Had something happened?" he says. "Was she upset about something?"

It doesn't seem to matter that I don't answer. He carries on talking anyway.

"I know her and Mum argue and stuff, but that's just normal isn't it?"

I nod.

"What could be this bad? I mean, she's quite nice looking, she's clever, everyone likes her! Shit! It's so out of character . . ."

The bus stops at the traffic lights beside school.

"There's a lot of pressure at school," I say.

"Anna wouldn't be worried by that!" says Tom dismissively. "She could get ten A grades standing on her head!"

"Perhaps that's the problem," I say. It isn't, of course. Or at least, not the whole of it.

Tom is drawing on the misted-up windows of the bus with his finger. "I bet Mum's going insane," he says.

"I think it might have something to do with Hayley Parkin," I say cautiously.

"That was all ages ago," says Tom. He rubs the glass with his palm, erasing the lines he has made. "Anyway Hayley's all right," he says.

I don't comment.

"She's just got a bit of a big mouth." Tom smiles to himself.

I think of the party.

"I can't see what Anna was making all the fuss about there," says Tom. "Hayley says it was just a bit of a joke. She really likes Anna . . ."

I want to say something in Anna's defence but I don't. What's the point?

We reach the hospital and the bus jerks to a stop.

53

It's about ten o'clock when Tom and I arrive at the hospital. When we get to Intensive Care Mrs Goldsmith is just coming out through the door. When she sees Tom, she starts to cry. He embraces her, swallowing her into a hug so that she looks like a tiny child.

"Tom, I thought she was dead," she says, pressing her face into his chest. "She looked as if *she* was dead. If I hadn't come back . . . if I hadn't gone to the loo . . . gone upstairs . . ." Her shoulders are shaking.

"It's OK, Mum," says Tom. "It'll be OK."

Frances sits down on a chair in the corridor. Tom crouches on the floor beside her and starts asking questions. "Is she still in a coma?"

Frances nods, then she says, "I think so . . . but she was waking up . . . starting to . . . that's what they said . . . they're monitoring her in case her heart goes funny . . . that's a risk . . . rhythm disturbance . . ."

"Where's Dad?"

"He's in there. With Anna. I only came out to go to the toilet . . ."

Mrs Goldsmith looks at me, standing behind Tom, fiddling with my hair.

"Hello, Melanie," she says. She wipes her eyes. "Thanks for coming."

I smile.

"So what happens next?" says Tom.

"We just wait," says Frances. She sighs. "We just go on waiting."

Frances Goldsmith starts fishing in her bag, as though she's looking for something. She pulls out a folded sheet of writing paper.

"This is for you, Melanie," she says. She hands it to me. I see my name written with Anna's fountain pen. "It was in the bathroom beside her. There's one for Hayley Parkin too."

"Oh," I say. I look at Tom.

"Was she in the bathroom?" Tom says.

Frances nods.

"Unconscious?" asks Tom.

Frances nods again. Then she says again, "I thought she was dead, Tom. I was sure she was dead." She grips his hand tighter and tears stream down her face.

We wait. Frances goes back in. Then Mr Goldsmith comes out and Tom goes in.

"How is she?" I say to Mr Goldsmith. He is still in his theatre clothes. He has dark rings under his eyes.

"She's stable," he says. He pushes his hair off his face.

"Is she . . . out of danger?" I ask. That's the phrase people use, isn't it? That's what they say on the News, in *Casualty* . . .

"Not yet," he says, peeling off rubber gloves. "I'm just going to get a coffee." He starts to walk away.

"Mr Goldsmith?" I say. I want to ask him if Anna is going to die, but it seems rather a tactless question so instead I just say, "I'm really sorry."

For a moment it looks as if he is going to cry. Then he turns and walks towards the cafeteria.

As I watch him go, I wonder what I will say if Anna dies. Anna Goldsmith was my friend. It has a hollow ring to it.

I don't read Anna's letter straight away. I stare at the rubber plant beside my chair and watch people using the chocolate machine further down the corridor. I am haunted by yesterday. By what I said. How I looked. How Anna must have felt . . .

It was Friday. Yesterday. March fourteenth.
Afternoon break, just before Maths. Anna was
supposed to be sleeping over on Saturday night.
Tonight, in fact. We'd arranged it ages ago. She was
going to come over this afternoon and we were going
to go into town, to go round the shops. Anna had
some clothes money to spend. She wanted a new top.

Anna was acting strange. More strange than usual.
She'd hardly spoken all day. At lunchtime she went
straight to the library and didn't have anything to
eat. In English I was telling her something about
orchestra but she wasn't listening. She looked as if
she was behind a pane of glass and she couldn't hear
me. I wanted to shake her.

"Are you OK?" I said, as we were walking along
the corridor.

"I found a poem," she said. "In the library. It
describes how I'm feeling . . ."

"Does that mean you're OK or not?" I said.

"My ankle still hurts," she said. I noticed she was
limping. "From when Hayley bashed me," she said.

That was over a week ago.

"Anna," I said, "it was an accident. I'm sure she
didn't mean to . . ." My words sounded empty and

meaningless. Who was I kidding?

Anna looked at me. "I suppose it was a joke," she said. "Sorry! I should have laughed. Ha-ha! Hilarious bruise! Really funny pain! Side-splitting, Melanie!"

We were outside Maths. Hayley was watching us. She was chewing gum, winding it round her finger.

"What time shall I come tomorrow?" I said, changing the subject. "To go into town?"

Anna didn't answer.

"Well how long do you want to be in town?" I asked.

Anna flicked her hair out of her eyes and yawned. "I don't fancy shopping any more," she said.

"I thought you wanted a new top?" I said.

"I changed my mind," Anna said.

Hayley caught my eye. "I'm going down town tomorrow, Mel. You could come with me," she said.

I didn't answer.

Anna wasn't looking at me. She was staring into space.

"What *do* you want to do then?" I asked her.

"I don't know."

She had her vague face on. I felt irritated.

"I don't want to just sit around talking about nothing!" I said.

"You're the one that talks about nothing," said Anna.

"What's that supposed to mean?" I said. I said

it too loud. Everyone heard.

"It means Anna thinks you're boring, Melanie," said Hayley. Then she said, "Let's face it . . . she's right!"

"Just shut up!" I said, looking at Hayley. I could feel myself going red. I was mad with Anna for making me look stupid so I said, "I suppose it's really interesting talking about death?" I was staring at Anna. "And bleeding . . . and falling into holes . . . and icebergs . . ." I couldn't stop – the words just tumbled out. "All this poor victim self-pity stuff!"

"Sounds like a bunch of laughs!" said Siobhan Reid.

Anna looked at me, willing me to stop.

"Anna isn't into laughs!" said Hayley. "Are you, Anna?"

"Shut up, Hayley. Keep out of this," I said.

"Let's just forget the sleepover, shall we?" said Anna.

I ignored her. I felt as though a firework was going off in my head.

"Do you think *you're* such brilliant company?" I said. I don't know why I said it. It was so cruel, so vicious. I kept on: "Do you think I enjoy sitting around listening to how unhappy you are? Looking at your dismal face? Lighten up, Anna! Get a life, will you!"

Hayley and Siobhan cheered.

"It's about time someone told her what a miserable cow she is!" Hayley said.

I wanted to smack her one.

Anna looked like a rabbit, caught in the headlights of a car. "I thought you were my friend," she said quietly.

"I thought you were mine," I shouted back. "It cuts both ways, Anna!"

She picked up her violin and ran down the corridor.

"Mind out!" yelled someone, as Anna crashed through the swing doors.

"Oops!" said Hayley Parkin. Then she smirked.

56

The letter isn't what I expected. I thought it would attack me, accuse me of betrayal. It doesn't. It should have done.

Dear Mel,
When you read this I will be dead.
You said I should lighten up, laugh things off more, not take life so seriously. I am sorry I couldn't do that. I am too small and the pain is too big.
I was wrong to expect you to understand me, but if anyone knows why I'm doing this, then you do, Melanie. You told me to get a life. I had one, but Hayley Parkin took it away from me.
Here is part of the poem I told you about – the one I found in the library. It's by Stevie Smith and it's called **Not waving, but Drowning***.*

Nobody heard him, the dead man,
But still he lay moaning:
I was much further out than you thought
And not waving but drowning...
...I was much too far out all my life
And not waving but drowning.

That's me, Mel. I'm too far out. Further out than
you thought.

   Thanks for being my friend.

   love, Anna xx

   PS. Tell Mum to let you have my mobiles. I know
how much you like them.

The poem sent shivers down my spine.

57

Tom comes out into the corridor. I am still holding the letter.

"Are you OK?" he says.

I sniff and nod my head.

"Mum says would you like to come in to see her?" says Tom. "It's supposed to be family only but the nurses said it was OK . . ."

I follow him through the doors.

Mr Goldsmith stands up. "I'll wait outside with Tom," he says. "It'll be a bit crowded otherwise . . ."

I walk to the end of the bed, not sure what I will see, and look at Anna. There is a needle in her arm and wires coming from her chest. But more than these I notice her hair, all splayed out on the pillow, and her skin like china – like one of those Victorian dolls. She looks really beautiful.

Frances is sitting by the bed. She looks much calmer again now. She smiles at me. "Have a seat," she says, touching the empty chair beside her.

I sit down. There is a huge lump in my throat and my palms are prickling. I think of Anna in the queue for Maths, her eyes wide and frightened. I see the sight of her back as she flees along the corridor – like an injured animal, running off to die alone.

A nurse comes to check Anna's temperature.

"This is Melanie," says Mrs Goldsmith. "Anna's best friend."

The nurse smiles at me.

Best friend. Some joke. Some friend. I feel like a traitor.

I watch the nurse reading the monitors and writing on a board.

"I didn't think she'd really do it," I say suddenly. "Not for real!" I cannot help myself. I begin to cry. "It's my fault," I say, between sobs. "It's my fault she did it!" Great fat tears splash on to my knees.

Mrs Goldsmith puts her hand on my arm. "Melanie," she says. "It's not your fault. You were her friend. You *are* her friend. You were the one that was there for her . . ."

"I said terrible things!" I say.

Mrs Goldsmith sighs deeply. "We all did," she says. "You mustn't blame yourself."

She hugs me, a little awkwardly. It makes me cry even more.

"Have a tissue," she says, rummaging in her bag. "I've been getting through box loads of them!" I blow my nose.

Anna rolls her leg to one side. The movement startles me.

"Is she going to be all right?" I ask.

"I hope so," says Frances. Then she says, "We're

all rooting for her, aren't we?"

I nod. I wish Anna could see us. I want her to know that I'm sorry.

"I wish she knew," I say. "I wish she could see us all here. You, and David and Tom . . ."

I look at Frances. She is watching Anna. She looks worn out. There are deep lines around her eyes – pain lines, like scars.

We sit in silence, then Frances says, "I've been reading Anna's diary." She takes the blue notebook out of her bag. I stare at it. Anna's so secretive about her diary. No one, but *no one*, gets to see it! She hides it in her drawer. Anna would be furious if she knew. I would be furious too, if it was me . . .

Frances reads my thoughts. "Does that make me a nosey cow?" she says. I blush. "If she'd died we would have read it," Frances says. "If I hadn't come back and found her. If I'd come home a couple of hours later, when she expected me to. Dead people don't have any secrets."

She has a point. When my grandma died, my mum read all her letters – even the really private ones.

"But it would have been too late then," says Frances. "Too late to learn from our mistakes. Too late to understand . . ."

I look at Anna's arms, at the mauve stripes criss-crossing her flesh.

"Do you ever wish you could un-say things?" I ask. "Like you had an erase button you could press and that bit never happened? Gone!" I press an imaginary button on my leg and make a buzzing sound.

Frances smiles briefly. "All the time," she says. "Sometimes I wish I could have the children as babies all over again. Start again with a clean sheet and make a better job of it. They should give you dummy children to practise on first – to make all your mistakes on – then you can have the real thing and do it right. Say all the right things . . ."

I wonder if my mum feels like that too.

"I wish I'd stuck up for Anna more," I say. "I was piggy in the middle. I was pathetic! I should have been stronger. I wish I'd stepped in more and not let Hayley Parkin . . ." I don't finish. I can't think what to say.

"Back you all into a corner," says Frances. She taps the cover of Anna's notebook. "It's all in here," she says. "I see it all as clear as day now. I only wish I'd read it months ago – or listened better. Listened at all. I had no idea how big it all was . . ."

"I was too small and the pain was too big," I say.

"Sorry?" says Frances, turning her head towards me.

"That was what Anna wrote in my letter," I say. I take the folded paper out of my pocket. "I was much further out than you thought," I read. "Not waving, but drowning."

"Thank God she didn't drown," says Mrs Goldsmith. She says it very quietly, under her breath.

"I hate Hayley Parkin," I say. It is the first time I've ever said it.

"Oooh . . ." Frances shudders. "Don't get me started," she says. She sighs a big sigh and closes her eyes. "I don't know how the hell I'm going to deliver this without landing her one!" she says, pulling Hayley's letter out of her bag. "That would put the icing on the cake wouldn't it? Teacher done for grievous bodily harm!"

"You could just put it in the bin," I say.

"No," says Frances. "I think Hayley needs to see it, don't you?"

I don't answer.

"Whatever it says." Frances smooths the paper with her fingers. "Anna took the trouble to write it . . ." Her voice trails off.

I look at Anna. I look at the letter. My heart is racing. I know what I have to do.

58

Hayley Parkin's house is on the hill behind the hospital. It's a good twenty minutes' walk and the road is steep and cobbled. I have to keep stopping to catch my breath. I have the letter in my hand. Folded yellow paper, just like mine, and Anna's handwriting, stylish and neat. I grip it tightly. My stomach is churning.

Halfway up the hill I sit down on a bench. I can see the whole town below me, like a model. I can see the park and our road and school and the shopping precinct. I can see the hospital with its grey chimney. I picture Anna in her bed, hooked up to all the contraptions, surrounded by numbers and charts and flashing lights. I am doing this for Anna. It's the least I can do.

Hayley's mother answers the door. She has a bathrobe on and a towel round her hair. It's the first time I've seen her with no make-up on. She looks even more like Hayley.

"Hello, Melanie," she says. She looks surprised to see me. "Is everything all right?"

I don't answer the question. "Is Hayley in?" I ask. I don't look at her. I don't want to lose my nerve.

"I think she's still in bed," she says. "I'll just give

her a shout. Come in Melanie."

I step into the hall. Mrs Parkin goes to the foot of the stairs.

"Hayley!" she calls.

There is a pause. Hayley doesn't answer.

"How's your mum?" says Mrs Parkin, making conversation.

"Fine," I say blankly. I catch sight of myself in the mirror in the hall. My face is really red and my hair is all over the place.

Mrs Parkin calls again, *"Hayley!"*

I hear Hayley's voice upstairs. Mrs Parkin glances at the piece of paper in my hand.

"It's for Hayley," I say.

"Well do you want to just leave it and I'll give it to her?"

"I'd like to give it to her myself, thanks," I say coldly.

"Well," she says. "You'd better go on up."

I climb the stairs, my feet sinking into the deep pile carpet. On the landing there are photographs of Hayley in gold frames: a whole series, starting with baby ones right up to last year's school photo. Hayley Parkin – her life in pictures. She looks the same in all of them. The baby-blonde hair, the perfect features, the healthy tan, the sickly smile. I've seen them often enough before but today they jump out at me. If I had a can of spray paint I would deface them all!

I knock on Hayley's bedroom door.

"Come in," she says.

I step inside. The curtains are still drawn. I can see Hayley's shape under the duvet. I switch on a light.

"Hello Hayley," I say.

She props herself up on her elbows. "What are you doing here?" she says.

"I brought you this," I say. "It's from Anna." I walk over to the bed and put the folded letter in her hands.

She smiles. "Have you and Anna kissed and made up after yesterday's little tiff then, Melanie?" she says, sitting up.

"I haven't spoken to her since," I say.

"I shouldn't think she wants to see you, Mel," says Hayley with a grin. Then she says, "You were such a cow yesterday! I didn't know you had it in you, Mel!"

I take a deep breath. "She took an overdose," I say.

Hayley stops grinning. "She what?"

"Anna took an overdose. Anna Goldsmith – remember her? That girl who used to be your friend." My voice is getting louder and louder as I speak. I stare at Hayley, drilling her with my eyes.

Suddenly Hayley laughs. "That's just the sort of over-the-top thing Anna Goldsmith would do, isn't it?" Then she says, "Oh dear, Melanie, I hope you don't feel too responsible, sticking the boot in like you did . . ."

"I'll leave the feeling responsible to you, Hayley," I say. Just for a moment I can see a flicker of panic go across her face. Then she smiles again.

"Come on Mel! You're not suggesting it was anything to do with me?"

She raises her eyebrows and smiles at me, like a dog when it's after your sandwiches.

"Mel?" she says. It comes out like a whimper.

"Read the letter," I say.

She looks at the paper, still folded on the bed and then she hands it back to me.

"You read it," she says. "Read it to me."

"No," I say, dropping it on the sheets.

"Mel, read it to me," says Hayley. She scowls at me like a spoilt child.

"No," I say again. It feels good to stand up to her. I feel as if I'm growing taller, like Alice in Wonderland. Soon I'll bang my head on the ceiling! "What are you so worried about?" I say. "If it's not your fault?"

Hayley picks up the letter. "What did she take?" she asks.

"Her mother's antidepressants. The ones you told her about. Remember?"

Hayley doesn't answer.

"And vodka," I say. "Gallons of it. She wanted to

do a proper job. She wasn't just playing at it, Hayley."

"Is she dead?" Her voice sounds like thin ice, just waiting to crack.

"Read the letter," I say, looking at the floor.

Does it make any difference if she is dead or alive? The damage is done. Hayley has done it. She opens the letter and reads it.

I know what it says because I read it while I sat on the bench looking down at the hospital. It wasn't sealed. It was only folded.

Hayley,

If I called you a murderer would that be too strong a word? By the time you read this I will be dead. That was what you wanted all along, wasn't it? To get rid of me completely. Character assassination, they call it.

I don't know what I ever did to make you hate me so much.

I don't know what went wrong. What made us enemies?

You have made me hate myself. You have made me feel worthless. You have made me want to die.

I hope that makes you feel good.

You did a good job, Hayley! I was your victim all right. You were like a spider devouring its prey.

I hope it tastes good, Hayley! Your victory.
I hope you don't regret it.
Your one-time friend,
Anna Goldsmith.

Hayley looks at the paper for a long time. I expected her to shout. Tear the letter up. Say it is all lies. Laugh it off. She doesn't. She just sits in silence.

For a moment, I almost feel sorry for her.

I walk towards the door. "Bye Hayley," I say.

She doesn't speak.

I am tempted just to go. Not tell her that Anna isn't dead. Not tell her that there's still time. I can't do it.

"Mrs Goldsmith found her in time," I say. "She's in the hospital, in Intensive Care." The door clicks shut behind me.

59

Frances Goldsmith stares at the ECG. Something is different. Something is wrong. The mountains are changing. They're not identical any more. Some are small. Some are large. There are jagged valleys, peaks, gaps, surges . . . "Nurse!"

The nurse is coming, moving very fast. "Get the defibrillator. She's gone into VF!"

"What's that?" Frances jumps to her feet.

They are moving machinery into place – more wires, more tubes, more numbers.

"Rhythm disturbance!" says the nurse.

"Oh God!" says Frances.

"I'm sorry, Mrs Goldsmith, would you mind just stepping outside a moment?" says the nurse. She is hooking up a drip stand.

Frances picks up her things.

"Can you bleep Dr Hurding?" says another nurse. There is panic in her voice. "Dr Hurding!" she says again.

Frances sees them slap two paddles on to Anna's chest. Anna twitches violently. Then the curtain swishes quickly round Anna's bed and Frances cannot see her any longer.

60

On the way back down the hill from Hayley's house I suddenly notice what a fantastic morning it is. The sky is really blue. The sun is sharp and bright. There are frost patterns on the stone wall beside the path in the nooks and crannies that the sun hasn't reached. In the gardens the bulbs are coming up, little bleached tips poking through the soil. I can hear birds singing, singing so loud it makes my head ring.

I am running downhill, slipping and sliding on the cobbles. I am running back to the hospital. Running back to Anna.

If I had some paper and a pen I would write her a letter but I haven't, so I write one in my head.

Dear Anna
Don't die. Too many people love you.
You weren't too far out, not too far out to be rescued.
Please don't die.
With love,
Your friend,
Melanie xx

61

Frances Goldsmith is in the corridor, clutching her things. David is coming back from the cafeteria with Tom. He sees his wife and walks faster.

"What's happened?" he shouts.

"Her heart went haywire!" says Frances. "VF they said . . ."

David Goldsmith is running. "How long ago?" he yells.

"Five minutes?" says Frances. "Maybe less . . ."

"If they'd given her the bloody Lignocaine this wouldn't have happened!" David is pushing open the door of Intensive Care.

"They won't let you in," says Frances feebly.

"Yes they will," says David. The door swings shut.

"Stay with me!" says Frances. She says it too late.

Tom puts his arms around her. She is white with panic.

"Tom . . . I'm so frightened . . ." she says.

62

It is lunchtime when I get back to the hospital. A nurse is wheeling a trolley load of shepherd's pie down the corridor. It smells like school dinners.

I feel a bit lightheaded and high. And I feel excited, as if something good is about to happen. A porter strides by, pushing an empty trolley. He is whistling. I feel like joining in.

I picture Anna as I walk. Her perfect skin and her hair, black against the pillow. I picture her waking up, opening her eyes, seeing the white ceiling, seeing the sunlight coming in above the blinds. I picture her smiling, seeing faces she knows. I am there beside her bed, and Frances and David and Tom. She is glad to wake up. She is glad that we are there.

I pass the chocolate machine. A woman is banging it with her fist and swearing. A boy with his leg in plaster goes by in a wheelchair. A teenage boy is pushing him. "Push it faster!" the boy says. "Make it do skids!" I laugh.

Then I am outside Intensive Care, in the corridor, beside the rubber plant. Frances is there, on the chairs where I sat before. Tom is there too. They have their heads bowed so I cannot see their faces.

"Hi," I say, brightly.

Tom looks up and I know straight away that something awful has happened.

I feel a wave of panic move across me like a dark shadow.

Frances is hunched in the chair with her eyes closed. She looks as if she is praying. Neither of them speak to me.

I stand in silence, not knowing what to ask. I am suddenly cold. I feel dizzy. I think I am going to fall over.

In my head I can hear myself yelling out, "*No! She's not dead! She can't be dead. Not Anna . . . She can't die . . . please no!*" I sink into one of the chairs.

Then Tom speaks, unsteadily, as if he will choke on the words, "Anna had . . . a sort of . . . heart attack . . . about half an hour ago . . ."

I nod. A heart attack. I try to imagine Anna's heart. A heart that has been attacked. Attacked by who? I imagine it wounded. Full of holes, as though it had been shot through with bullets, or arrows. Is this what they mean by a broken heart? Anna's heart is bleeding and they cannot make it stop. I remember Anna bleeding on to the bathroom tiles. Rivers of crimson.

I try to picture the doctors, behind the doors, behind the rectangles of frosted glass. What are they doing? What are they doing to Anna? Can they fix her heart? I pray that they can. Patch it up. Plug the holes. Make it work again. Make Anna well . . .

We sit in silence and nothing happens. There is a clock on the wall. I watch the pointers move. It is 1.33pm. The floortiles are black and white squares, like a chessboard. I start counting the squares, doing sums in my head. Anything to drown out the thoughts, to squash out the fear . . .

We have been sitting here forever and now David Goldsmith is coming through the doors. He looks exhausted. His face is blank. It gives nothing away. I can hardly bear to look at him.

Tom is standing up. "Have a seat, Dad," he is saying. He is moving to one side.

David is slumping into the empty chair, wrapping his arm around Frances. I can hear him speaking, speaking about Anna. "She's stabilised again," he is saying. "Anna's OK. I think she's going to be OK . . ."

I am staring at the black and white tiles but I cannot see them for tears. Wiping my face, I look up, out of the window. A bird flies by, darting and swooping across a rectangle of hazy blue.

What makes a gifted and attractive 16 year old hate herself? How can her self-esteem be so badly shredded that she wants to end her life? This was my starting point for writing BLUE. I wanted to explore the reality behind newspaper headlines about bullying and teenage suicide. Writing BLUE was harrowing at times but I hope it gives girls like Anna a voice – and some sense of being understood.

Sue Mayfield is the author of I CARRIED YOU ON EAGLES' WINGS and HANDS IN CONTRARY MOTION.

Acknowledgments

The writing of *Blue* grew out of a series of lunchtime workshops at The Crossley Heath School, Halifax in 1996. I am grateful for the valuable insights of Jo Sheridan, Nikola Butler, Annwen Parry, Sarah Rawlinson. Jenny Harvey, Helen Webster and Anna Wickenden who worked with me to develop the plotline and characters and who read (and greatly improved!) the first draft of the novel.

Special thanks to the staff of The Crossley Heath School, for enabling me to work with these students, to Liz Procter and Cathy Gunningham for medical advice and to my agent Elizabeth for her persistence and support.

All the characters and situations in *Blue* are fictional. Any resemblance to real people or places is unintentional.

Grateful thanks to the Estate of James MacGibbon for permission to reproduce an extract from "*Not Waving But Drowning*" by Stevie Smith.

NOSTRADAMUS AND INSTANT NOODLES

John Larkin

Ian Champion's mum and dad came to parenthood late – and by accident. It wasn't a good start and now – fourteen years later – his parents have had enough.

Suddenly from Sydney and its sun, sand and surf, Ian finds himself staying with relatives in chilly Yorkshire, faced with football, flatcaps and flooding.

This is what happens when your parents leave home before you do . . .

FESTIVAL

David Belbin

The Glastonbury Festival. Three days in June. For many, it's the event of the summer – for three Glastonbury virgins and one fourteen-year-old veteran, it's going to be a life-changing experience.

Leila, exams over, just wants to have fun. But first she has to find a way to get there . . .

Jake is playing the festival. This could be his big break. Or his biggest nightmare . . .

Wilf is forced to sell his ticket, so his only way in is to jump the fence. And there's a big surprise waiting on the other side . . .

Holly gets in free. It's her tenth Glastonbury. She's promised herself it'll be the last . . .

SPEAK

Laurie Halse Anderson

'. . . *I wasted the last weeks of August watching bad cartoons. I didn't go to the mall, the lake, or the pool, or answer the phone. I have entered high school with the wrong hair, the wrong clothes, the wrong attitude. And I don't have anyone to sit with.*'

From her first moment at Merryweather High, Melinda Sordino knows she's an outcast. Her old friends won't talk to her, and people she doesn't know glare at her. If only she could explain to them . . . but she just can't find the words.

'*The plot is gripping and the characters powerfully drawn . . . makes this a novel that will be hard for readers to forget.*' KIRKUS REVIEWS

ORDER FORM

Also available in the  series

0 340 81732 1	Nostradamus and Instant Noodles *John Larkin*	£4.99	❏
0 340 81746 1	Festival *David Belbin*	£4.99	❏
0 340 81762 3	Speak *Laurie Halse Anderson*	£4.99	❏
0 340 84148 6	Magenta Orange *Echo Freer*	£4.99	❏
0 340 80520 X	Four Days Till Friday *Pat Moon*	£4.99	❏

All Hodder Children's books are available at your local bookshop, or can be ordered direct from the publisher. Just tick the titles you would like and complete the details below. Prices and availability are subject to change without prior notice.

Please enclose a cheque or postal order made payable to *Bookpoint Ltd*, and send to: Hodder Children's Books, 130 Milton Park, Abingdon, OXON OX14 4SB, UK. Email Address: orders@bookpoint.co.uk

If you would prefer to pay by credit card, our call centre team would be delighted to take your order by telephone. Our direct line *01235 400414* (lines open 9.00 am–6.00 pm Monday to Saturday, 24 hour message answering service). Alternatively you can send a fax on *01235 400454*.

TITLE		FIRST NAME		SURNAME	

ADDRESS	

DAYTIME TEL:		POST CODE	

If you would prefer to pay by credit card, please complete:
Please debit my Visa/Access/Diner's Card/American Express (delete as applicable) card no:

Signature .... Expiry Date: ....

If you would NOT like to receive further information on our products please tick the box. ❏